KB085291

명두

아시아에서는 《바이링궐 에디션 한국 대표 소설》을 기획하여 한국의 우수한 문학을 주제별로 엄선해 국내외 독자들에게 소개합니다. 이 기획은 국내외 우수한 번역가들이 참여하여 원작의 품격을 최대한 살렸습니다. 문학을 통해 아시아의 정체성과 가치를 살피는 데 주력해 온 아시아는 한국인의 삶을 넓고 깊게 이해하는 데 이 기획이 기여하기를 기대합니다.

Asia Publishers presents some of the very best modern Korean literature to readers worldwide through its new Korean literature series ⟨Bilingual Edition Modern Korean Literature⟩. We are proud and happy to offer it in the most authoritative translation by renowned translators of Korean literature. We hope that this series helps to build solid bridges between citizens of the world and Koreans through a rich in-depth understanding of Korea.

바이링궐 에디션 한국 대표 소설 078

Bi-lingual Edition Modern Korean Literature 078

Relics

구효서
명두

Ku Hyo-seo

ASIA
PUBLISHERS

Contents

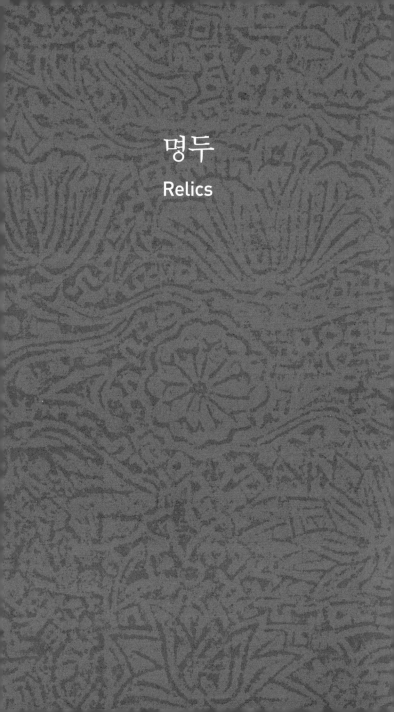

명두

Relics

나는 죽었다. 죽은 몸으로 20년을 서 있다. 잎이 없을 뿐, 생김새는 살아 있을 때와 별반 다를 게 없다. 철 따라 돋고 지던 잎들이 없어지니 외려 모양은 사시장철 여일해서 사람들이 기억하기엔 좋다. 이 마을에 태어나 서른 넘게 살아온 사람들은 나를 굴참나무로 기억한다.

처음 마주친 사람들은 한결같이 기분 나쁘다는 듯 나를 곁눈으로 흘겨보는데, 더러는 슬금슬금 다가와 표피를 만지거나 두드리면서 무슨 나무야? 라고 중얼거린다. 그러곤 내 죽음의 기운이 손끝에라도 번져갔을까 봐 슬그머니 손을 털거나 인상을 찡그리며 허리춤에 문

I am dead. I've been standing here dead for twenty years. I don't have leaves anymore, but my appearance hasn't changed much besides that. It's actually easier for people to remember me now, since my leaves don't sprout and fall with the seasons anymore. I look the same throughout the year. Villagers who've lived here their entire lives remember me as an oak tree.

Strangers cast disapproving glances at me. Some approach cautiously and touch my bark or give it a knock muttering, "What kind of tree is this?" And as if death had just rubbed off on their fingertips, they either dust off their hands discreetly or wipe their

지른다. 내가 무슨 나무인지 그들은 끝내 알아내지 못한다. 더 알려고도 하지 않는다. 그들에게 나는 그저 죽은 나무일 뿐이다. 무기물인 죽은 나무에게 사실 수종 따위 무슨 소용이겠는가.

20년 전 여름만 해도 나는 제법 무성한 이파리를 달고 있었다. 다른 나무들처럼 봄에는 잎을 틔우고 여름에는 우거지고 가을에는 낙엽을 떨구며 평온한 수목의 나날을 보냈다. 그러던 어느 날 갑작스레 이 빈촌에 대대적인 개발 바람이 불어닥쳤다. 산자락에 있던 판자촌이 통째로 부서지고, 산뜻한 콘크리트 마을이 산중턱에 새로 생기게 되면서 내 발목 아래로 큰길이 뚫렸다. 마을을 내려다보던 나는 어느 날부턴가 마을을 올려다보게 되었다. 숲에 있던 나는 졸지에 황량한 길가로 나앉게 되었던 것이다.

명두집이 아니었다면 그때 나는 아예 밑동이 잘려지거나 뿌리째 뽑혀 흔적 없이 사라졌을 것이다. 명두집이 나서서 온몸으로 나를 지켰다. 나를 살리기 위해 그녀는 목숨을 걸었다. 그리하여 훤하게 뚫린 산작로변에 나홀로 꼴사납게 서 있게 되었다.

back pockets, looking disgruntled. They never figure out what kind of tree I am, nor do they try. To them, I'm just a dead tree. What's the use paying a dead tree any attention?

Twenty summers ago I was quite the leafy tree. Still, I was mostly like any other tree. I budded in the spring, grew lots of leaves in the summer, and shed my leaves in the autumn. It was a peaceful life. Then, a huge development boom hit our slum of a village. They crushed our shantytown at the foot of the mountain and erected an immaculate village of concrete higher up. They paved a large road in front of my ankles. I used to peer down at the village; now I had to look up to see it. I ended up alone on a dreary roadside, no longer part of the forest.

If it weren't for the Myeongdu Lady, they would've chopped me down or uprooted me. Gone without a trace. She stood up for me and guarded me with her whole body, risking her own life to save mine. That's how I ended up sticking out like a sore thumb on the side of the wide new road. A large oak tree by the road would have been a natural beauty at least, but the builders would have to re-direct the road in order to save me, and someone

새로 난 길가에 우뚝 서 있는 커다란 굴참나무 한 그루는 나름대로 자연미가 있어 그윽하게도 보였겠으나, 나무를 살리기 위해서는 부득이 도로의 진행 방향을 약간 틀어야만 했고, 그로 인해 손해를 보는 사람이 생겼던 것이다. 집 앞으로 도로가 나면 멋진 가든을 지어 돼지갈비로 부자가 되고팠던 그 사람은 내 모양이 꼴사나울 수밖에 없었다. 나무가 죽어버리면 기존의 계획대로 다시 도로를 내주지 않을까 싶었던 그는, 어느 날 밤 내 밑동에다 두 개의 드릴 구멍을 내고 한쪽에는 가루후추 네 통을, 다른 구멍에는 제초제 두 병을 쏟아 부었다.

 그래서 나는 그해 여름 죽게 되었는데, 도로는 끝내 새로 나지 않았다. 명두집이 죽은 나를 끌어안고 끝까지 버텼기 때문이다. 마을에서 그녀를 말릴 사람은 아무도 없었다. 살아서 150년, 죽어서 20년을 나는 한자리에 서 있다.

 내 주변은 풀밭이다. 뱀처럼 굽은 가느다란 외길이 풀밭 사이를 건너와 수줍은 듯 내 발치에 와 닿으며 멈춘다. 반대쪽 길 끝은 저만치 사철나무 담장 밖으로 사라

was not happy about that. That someone was set on becoming rich with all the traffic that the new road would bring to his house. He would build a handsome garden in the front yard and sell pork ribs, but I ruined his moneymaking schemes. One night, hoping they'd go back to their initial plan if I were dead, he drilled two holes in my lower trunk and dumped four tubs of ground pepper in one and two bottles of weed killer in the other.

So I died that summer, but they didn't change the road. It was all thanks to the Myeongdu Lady. She wrapped her arms around me and refused to let go until she won. No one in the village could talk her out of it. That's how I came to stand in the same spot; alive for 150 years, dead for twenty.

Grass grows around me. A serpentine path winds its way through the grass and stops timidly at my feet. The other end of the path disappears behind the wall of spindle trees in the distance.

They planted the grass after laying the big asphalt road. There was no path then. Two years later, for no reason, they stopped landscaping the facilities. Dandelion spores landed and took root in the grass; creeping lettuce and daisy fleabane began to

진다.

큰 아스팔트 길이 날 때 내 주변은 온통 잔디로 단장되었다. 그때는 물론 가느다란 외길이 나 있지 않았다. 이태 뒤 아무런 이유 없이 조경 시설에 대한 관리가 중단되었다. 민들레 홀씨가 날아들어 뿌리를 내렸고 씀바귀와 개망초가 싹을 틔웠다. 금강아지풀과 바랭이와 잠자리피가 웃자랐다. 봄에는 풀 사이로 민들레가, 여름에는 씀바귀가, 가을에는 구절초가 꽃을 피웠다. 다른 풀들에게 자리를 내어주긴 했어도 잔디는 잔디대로 꾸준히 자랐다. 풀과 꽃과 잔디가 자라는 동안 시나브로 외길도 숨을 쉬듯 조금씩 자라났다. 하루도 빼놓지 않고 나에게 다녀가는 발길이 그 길을 키웠다. 한 사람의 발길이었으므로 길은 어느 정도 이상 살이 찌지 않았고 차라리 위태로웠다. 그래도 그 길이 있어서 주변의 꽃들과 풀들이 더 다정하거나 아름답게 보였다. 나를 오가는 발길이었으나 발길의 주인공은 주변의 풀꽃들에게도 사랑의 눈길을 던지는 걸 늘 잊지 않았으므로.

명두집. 그러나 그녀는 오늘 내게 오지 않을 것이다. 20년 동안, 내가 숲에 있었을 때까지 친다면 무려 50년

sprout. Golden bristle grass, crabgrass, and oat grass flourished. Dandelions sprouted between the blades of grass in spring and creeping lettuce in the summer. Siberian chrysanthemums blossomed in autumn. The grass made room for the weeds but still managed to thrive on its own. As the weeds and the flowers and the grass grew, the path surfaced little by little in search of air. The footprints that came to see me each day widened the path. The footprints belonged to just one person, so the path didn't get any wider after a certain point. It was feeble, but it made the surrounding flowers and grasses more beautiful and approachable. The path led to me, but I always knew that the owner of the footprints also admired the flowers on the way.

The Myeongdu Lady. She will not come today. My daily visitor of twenty years—close to fifty if you count my forest years—will stop coming from this day forward.

She came to see me in the rain and the snow. When she was sick, her steps were like slow-moving hands on a clock. During droughts, she carried a jug of water on her head and poured it at my feet. On holidays or exorcism days, she brought

가까이 하루도 멈추지 않았던 그녀의 발길이 마침내 오늘로써 끊길 것이기에.

눈이 오나 비가 오나 그녀는 나에게 다녀갔다. 몸이 아플 때는 시곗바늘처럼이나 느린 걸음으로 다녀갔다. 가뭄 때는 작은 물동이를 들고 와 발치에 부었고, 명절 때나 굿풀이를 한 날에는 사과와 배를 들고 찾았다. 이 마을 출신의 한 영화감독 지망생이 말했다. 죽은 나무에 3년 동안 물을 주어 열매를 맺게 했다는 전설 같은 얘기가 있지. 러시아 저명한 감독의 마지막 영화에도 그 얘기가 나와……. 그러나 명두집은 죽은 나무에 새 순이 나게 해달라거나 열매를 맺게 해달라는 비손을 한 적이 없었다. 그녀는 그냥 왔고, 왔다가 그냥 갔다. 그러기를 한평생. 마침내 그녀는 오늘 늙어 죽으려는 것이다. 나처럼 죽은 몸이 되려는 것이다. 그녀는 사람이라서, 나처럼 죽었으면서도 사시장철 여일하게 서 있지는 못할 것이다. 어쨌거나 그녀도 이제 나와 같은 죽음의 세계에 비로소 편입되려는 것이다. 몇 명의 마을 아낙이 조금 전 그녀의 집으로 황급히 달려갔다. 그녀의 일평생을 고스란히 지켜봤던 나였지만, 아니 그런 나였으

16

apples and pears. An aspiring film director from the village told this almost legendary story of a woman who watered a dead tree for three years and brought it back to life. He said a distinguished Russian film director had included that story in his last film. But the Myeongdu Lady never prayed for new buds or new shoots. She just came, and then left. Every single day. And today, at long last, she is dying of old age. She'll be a dead body like me, but because she's human, she won't be able to stay in one place over the years. In any case, she, too, will be brought into the world of death. Some of the village women rushed to her house not too long ago. Although I was there for the entirety of her life —rather, *because* I was there—I did not have the same sense of urgency they did.

Nobody knows. Except, perhaps, the trees that once made up the forest with me. None of the villagers know. The Myeongdu Lady buried three babies under me. None of them had made it past ten days. She buried the first baby under my southern roots, the second under my northern roots, and the third under my eastern roots.

Surely I noticed her lower belly swell. Then, it

므로, 저들처럼 다급한 맘이 생기지는 않는다.

　아무도 모르는 얘기다. 나와 함께 숲을 이루었던 나무들이라면 알까, 마을 사람 그 누구도 모르는 얘기다. 명두집은 내 밑동에다 세 아이를 묻었다. 모두 생후 열흘도 채 안 된 아이들이었다. 첫아이의 시신은 남쪽으로 난 뿌리 밑에, 나머지 두 아이는 각각 북쪽과 동쪽 뿌리 아래 묻혔다.

　그녀의 아랫배가 부풀어 오르는 것조차 모르지는 않았다. 부풀어 오르던 배는 어느 날 시나브로 꺼졌고, 마을 아낙들도 그녀의 배가 언제쯤 꺼질지 모두 짐작하고 있는 듯했다. 다만 세상 밖으로 나온 아이가 어디로 갔는지 모를 뿐이었다.

　산중턱에 새로운 주거단지가 생기기 전에는 많은 다른 수종들과 함께 나는 숲 속에 있었다. 쪼그려 앉으면 왜소한 여인 하나쯤 감쪽같이 숨길 만한 숲이었다. 게다가 그녀가 미친 듯이 내 밑동의 흙을 파냈을 때는 언제나 한밤중이었다. 갓난아이 하나 묻으려 파기에는 흙은 너무도 부드러웠고 그녀의 손가락은 온전한 갈퀴였

would stop growing one day and slowly deflate. Even the village women expected her stomach to die down at some point. They just didn't know where her babies went after they left her womb.

Before they built the residential complex on the mountainside, I made up a forest with many other trees. It was dense enough to completely hide a small woman if she crouched. When she came to dig, it was always in the middle of the night. The soil was all too soft to bury a newborn, and her fingers were perfect for the job. She waited for a moonless night to bury the baby, which she laid flat on its stomach the morning of. She trekked up the mountain in pitch darkness and dug the soil up beneath me like a mad woman. I remember shuddering when the child's body heat touched my roots once.

She had two children already around the ages of ten. When her first-born daughter turned eight, she gave her away to a family on the other side of the mountain. The girl would watch children for Mr. Kwak's second wife. Mr. Kwak's great-great-grandfather was famed in that region for barely passing the civil service examination. The Myeong-du Lady's son would follow his father from an early

다. 그녀는 달빛 없는 날을 헤아려 아침부터 아이를 엎어놓았다. 그러곤 칠흑 같은 산길을 헤집고 올라와 화가 난 사람처럼 식식거리며 내 발치의 흙을 파헤쳤다. 채 가시지 않은 아이의 체온이 뿌리에 닿을 때 나는 부르르 진저리를 친 적도 있었다.

그녀에겐 이미 열 살 안팎의 아이가 둘이나 있었다. 맏딸은 여덟 살 되던 해 이미, 5대조가 겨우 초시에 합격했었다는 산 너머 곽씨네 둘째 마나님의 애보기로 주어버리곤 그만이었다. 사내아이는 아비와 함께 일찌감치 품앗이를 다니거나 송기를 베거나 하릴없이 싸리나무 빗자루를 만들거나 했는데, 가난하기로 치자면 마을 사람 전부가 다 거기가 거기여서 그들에게 품을 나누어 줄 여유조차 없었다. 굶는 사람 살리자고 그들 부자에게 일부러 없는 품을 만들어 주었다가는 자기가 굶어야 할 판이었다. 자기 땅이라곤 한 뼘도 없을뿐더러, 소작부칠 땅조차 구할 수 없는 툇골이었다. 사연만 많고 집은 없는 뜨내기들이 하나둘씩 오가다 꼽사리로 끼어들며 만들어진 마을이라 해마다 좁쌀 됫박이나마 바치지 않으면 산림주로부터 쫓겨나기 일쑤였다.

age to help out on other farms, trim pines, or, when there was nothing else left to do, fashion brooms from bush clover branches. In terms of poverty, the villagers were not much better off themselves, so no one could afford outside help on their farms. A family that offered work to the starving father and son would have to go hungry themselves to compensate for the labor. The inhabitants of the makeshift village owned not a scrap of land to their name nor could they find any to lease. The village was formed when one a stray wanderer, rich with misfortune but poor as a pauper, settled in the nooks and crannies of the mountainside. They lived on the verge of expulsion by the mountain land's owner for as long as they could remember. They appeased him with, at the very least, a basket of millet each year.

The adjacent villages didn't fare any better. One nearly had to walk to the point of starvation before even catching sight of a thatched house with a proper roof. And even among the lucky ones who grew to adulthood in the village, only a few would ever see a tiled roof in their entire lifetimes. The stream was constantly abuzz with people trying to relieve their hunger, but none drank their fill lest it

인근 마을의 사정이라봤자 나을 게 없었다. 허기가 지도록 걸어나가야 고작 지붕을 제대로 얹은 초가를 볼 수 있었다. 툇골에서 태어나 운 좋게 목숨을 부지한 사람조차도 평생 기와집 구경을 못 해본 사람이 태반이었다. 배를 채우려는 사람들로 샘물가엔 사람이 끊이지 않았으나 그나마 체면 때문에 실컷 마시지도 못했다. 누군지도 모른 채, 입을 덜자고 무작정 어린 자식을 타지 사람의 손에 딸려 보내거나, 끼니 굶지 않는 집이라 하여 열다섯도 안 된 계집아이를 애 줄줄이 딸린 홀아비의 재취로 들여보냈다. 툇골에서 태어나 그렇게 마을을 떠났던 쉰여섯 살의 애봉이라는 여자가 최근 아침 텔레비전 방송에서 마흔네 해 만에 동생을 만나 펑펑 울기도 했다.

태어나자마자 죽지 않더라도, 많은 아이들이 열 살도 되기 전에 병으로 죽거나 굶어 죽었다. 그런데도 살아 있다는 이유로 여자들의 배는 쉼 없이 부르고 꺼졌다. 그러나 좀처럼 툇골의 인구는 늘지 않았다. 죽거나 버려지거나 어딘가로 보내졌다. 자식을 낳아 죽이고 버리며 한스럽게 나이를 먹은 사람들은 다 늙기도 전에, 간

give away how hungry they really were. It wasn't uncommon to send a young child off with a complete stranger from another town, or marry off a young girl to a widower with children before she even turned fifteen, because *that* household had enough to eat. It was one less mouth to feed. The now 56-year-old Aebong was one of those girls. She cried her eyes out when she was recently reunited on TV with her younger sister after 44 years.

Many of the babies who survived infancy died of disease or starvation before the age of ten. The women knew that, but because they were human, their bellies continued to swell and disappear, swell and disappear. However, the village population didn't grow. Children died, were abandoned, or were sent somewhere. The villagers grew old, but always burdened with the remorse of killing or abandoning their children. The children who managed to grow to adulthood left their old parents to die before they could properly age. Some went senile at the age of sixty and froze to death in the winter or drowned in the water. There were too many births and too many deaths to celebrate or mourn anything. They believed everything happened according to the will of the Grandmother of

신히 목숨을 연명한 자식들에 의해 죽임을 당하고 버려졌다. 나이 예순이면 망령이 들어 얼어 죽거나 물에 빠져 죽도록 방치되었다. 너무 많이 태어나고 너무 많이 죽어서, 기쁘거나 슬퍼할 겨를이 없었다. 모든 게 삼신할미의 조화며 염라대왕의 뜻이었다. 아이가 일찍 죽어 없어져 버리면 누군가가 그 삼신할미 허리띠 참 되게 짧았나 보네, 라고 선창했고, 나머지 사람들은 그려 그런가 뵈, 라고 합창하듯 따라하고는 잊어버렸다. 먹은 게 부실한 늙은이가 소리 없이 말라 죽어도 아따 염라대왕 그 양반 성질도 급하시지, 라는 식으로밖에 말할 줄 몰랐다. 그렇게 말하던 사람 중에는 귀신에 씌거나 미쳐서 갑자기 죽는 사람도 있었다. 그리고 죽은 사람은 곧 다 잊혀졌다. 지금은 이런 일들을 고릿적 얘기로 취급하지만, 사실 먼 얘기도 남의 얘기도 아니었다.

제 입조차 추스를 수 없었던 명두집 내외는 딸아이 하나를 남의 집 애보기로 진작에 버렸고, 남아 있는 사내아이마저 밥 먹듯 굶겼다. 내외의 형편은 말할 것도 없었다. 그런데도 해가 바뀌어 샘가에 감이 열리면 명두집의 허기진 뱃속에도 아이가 들어찼고, 감이 떨어지

24

Birth and the King of Hell. When a child died young, someone would remark, "The Grandmother of Birth, her belt must've been real short this time."

The rest would respond in unison, "Yeah, that's probably right," and the incident would be forgotten soon after.

When an older villager died from malnutrition, the others would say something along the lines of, "The King of Hell sure is impatient, isn't he?"

That's the only way they knew how to interpret death. Among such commenters, some would later find themselves possessed or would die from a sudden madness. The dead were not remembered for long. Such happenings were talked about as tales from the past, but they are still just as relevant today.

Barely able to appease their own stomachs, the Myeongdu Lady and her husband were quick to give their daughter away to a complete stranger while they starved their son—the only child they had left—as if it was their job. Their dire circumstances spoke for themselves. Still, whenever the year changed and the persimmon trees by the stream bore fruit, the Myeongdu Lady's withered belly also continued to bear children. And when

면 아이도 툭 하고 가랑이 사이에서 떨어졌다. 그렇게 둘이나 되는 아이를 떫은 감 버리듯 내 발치에 묻을 동안, 그녀의 남자는 두 번 다 곯은 배를 끌어안고 움막 안에 시체처럼 널브러져 있었다. 마지막으로 묻은 아이는 그녀의 남편이 뱀에 물려 죽은 뒤 두 해나 지나서 생긴, 아비를 알 수 없는 애였다.

다른 마을 다른 집들의 지붕이 명두집에 비해 다소 고요했다 하여 그 속사정까지 다를 수는 없었다. 셋까지는 아니었더라도, 너나없이 가난한 데다 너나없이 긴 긴 밤은 참을 수 없었으므로 집집마다 원치 않는 아이들이 생기고 없어지기 마련이었다. 다만 각자 나름대로 삼신할미와 염라대왕의 명호를 은밀히 외우며 처리해 잘 모를 뿐이었다. 공범의식 때문에 서로 묻지 않는 거였으면서, 사람들은 그런 일에 대해 물으면 지신이 성을 내 동티가 난다는 오래된 금기를 명분으로 지켰다. 가난과 허기에서 벗어나지 못하는 한 죽음에 대한 중압감은 일상적인 거였고 때로는 시시각각 아주 예리한 칼날처럼 그들을 위협했다. 그럴 때마다 도망치듯, 혹은 죽음을 앞당기듯, 아니면 대책 없는 습관처럼 곁에 있

the persimmons dropped from the branches, the baby, too, fell from between her legs. While she buried two of those babies, tossed out like unripe persimmons, her husband lay like a corpse in their mud hut, clenching his hollow stomach. The third and last baby she buried was conceived two years after snakes killed her husband; the father of the baby was never known.

Things may have been more tranquil under the other village roofs, but the circumstances couldn't have been much different. Everyone was poor and no one could restrain themselves in the long, long night. Naturally, unwanted babies were conceived and done away with—as many as three for some families. They called on the Grandmother of Birth and the King of Hell as they performed the deed in secret so the other villagers wouldn't be aware of what they had done. It was taboo to ask, anyways, because of the old belief that asking would incur the wrath of the Earth God. But the real reason for their silence was the guilt they felt knowing they were not ones to speak.

As long as they stayed trapped in the throes of poverty and hunger, death pressured them daily, at times threatening them like a sharp knife blade to

는 사람을 숨가쁘게 얼싸안았고, 당연한 결과로 불행이 예고된 새 생명이 탄생했다. 죽음은 끝없이 생명을 만들고, 삶은 끝없이 죽음을 낳았다.

그러니까 아무도 모르는 얘기가 아니라, 마을 사람 누구나 다 아는 얘기였다. 은밀히 처리한 날짜와 장소를 모를 뿐이었다. 자신들만 알고 있다가 그마저도 잊었다. 애써 죽음을 잊고자 하니 마침내는 날짜와 장소마저 까마득히 잊었던 것이다. 여기저기 묻었고, 묻은 곳에 또 묻었다. 산 사람들은 죽은 자의 땅을 밟거나 베고 살아간다는 사실을 몰랐다. 알려고도 하지 않았다.

그러나 명두집은 잊지 않았다. 50년 동안 하루도 잊은 날이 없었다. 묻어버리고 잊어버리며 나이를 먹어간 사람들이 몰랐을 뿐이다. 그녀가 세 아이를 내 발치에 묻었다는 사실을.

몰랐던 이유 중 하나는 낭설 때문이었다. 명두집은 아이를 땅에 묻지 않고 옹기에 담아두었다는 소문이 돌았다. 그녀가 귀신 쒼 사람을 고치고 미친 사람을 다스리는 놀라운 영험을 보이기 시작하면서 으스스한 소문이

the throat at any variable moment. And whenever it did, they thrust their bodies at their partners in an attempt to run away from death, to expedite it, or just simply out of reckless habit. Naturally, this resulted in the birth of yet another new life. Death created life to no end, and life gave birth to death in the same manner.

It was no secret. The villagers knew. What they didn't know was when and where the secret deed was done. Only the deed-doers knew, but they eventually forgot. Because they tried to forget these deaths, they also completely forgot the dates and the locations of their secrets. Babies were buried here and there, sometimes in the same spot. The mountain folk did not know they were treading on lands belonging to the dead or that they lived amongst them. Nor did they care to know.

But the Myeongdu Lady didn't forget. Not a day in 50 years did she forget. It was those who grew older and forgot the babies they buried who didn't know that she had buried three children beneath me.

Rumors explained their ignorance. It was said that the Myeongdu Lady stored her babies inside earth-

생겼다.

영험 있는 자들이 죽은 자의 신체 일부를 품속에 간직한다는 소리는 오래된 얘기였다. 억울한 한을 품고 죽은 사람의 것일수록 효험이 있다고 했다. 세상 시름을 겪을 만큼 겪고 죽은 사람의 것은 효과가 없었다. 살고 죽는 게 시큰둥해져서 억울할 것도 한을 품을 것도 없었을 테니까. 모진 한을 품어야만 오래도록 중음을 떠돌며 인간계를 끈질기게 간섭할 수 있는 거였다. 세상 시름을 적게 겪었으되 몹시 애매하고 억울한 죽음이어야 포한의 순도가 높아졌다. 한을 품고 죽은 어린아이가 안성맞춤이었다. 영험을 얻은 사람은 그래서 새소리 같은 어린아이의 음성으로 사람의 병을 고치고 다스리기 마련이었다. 그런 죽음과의 만남은 그러나 요행에 기댈 수밖에 없었는데, 언제까지고 기다릴 수만은 없는 거였다. 만들어야 했다. 명두집도 그렇게 만들어 가졌다는 것이 소문의 내용이었다.

아이에게 젖을 먹이지 않는다. 금방 태어난 아이는 굶겨도 금방 죽지 않는다. 사나흘이 지나면 비로소 아이가 사지를 버르적거리며 죽을 듯이 운다. 그럴 때 어두

enware jars instead of burying them in the ground.
These sinister rumors about her spread when she
started to drive out demons and heal the insane.

It was an old tale that those with spiritual powers
kept a limb or body part of the dead somewhere
on them. This part of the body was believed to
have more potency if it once belonged to a child
who'd died an unfortunate death. If the person had
wrestled with life long enough, the body part
wouldn't be as useful because life and death would
no longer faze them by that time; they wouldn't die
with great regrets or sadness. Only those who died
with deep resentment were given time between
death and rebirth into the next life and could inter-
vene in the mortal realm. The resentment was val-
ued as more pure if the death was unknown and
unwanted. Dead babies were then a perfect source
of power. That's why those with spiritual powers
used a singsong, childlike voice to heal people.
Encountering a death like that requires luck—but
you can't wait around for luck to strike. You have
to create it yourself. And that's how, according to
all the rumors, the Myeongdu Lady came to possess her powers.

The villagers believed she didn't breastfeed her

운 항아리에 처넣고 뚜껑을 닫는다. 아이는 허기와 어둠과 한기에 갇혀 죽음을 직감한다. 그렇게 하루 이틀을 더 보내고 나면 아무리 갓난아이라 할지라도 바깥으로 나오려고 맹렬히 뚜껑을 밀친다. 커다란 돌을 뚜껑 위에 얹는다. 세상 경험을 전혀 하지 못한 아이의 공포는 그만큼 순명하다. 마침내 돌을 얹은 뚜껑마저도 들썩거린다. 잘 벼린 창칼을 들고 있다가 뚜껑 사이로 비어져 나온 손가락 하나를 단숨에 끊는다. 아이는 항아리의 어둠 속으로 굴러 떨어지며 발악을 한다. 몇 개의 돌을 더 뚜껑 위에 얹는다. 아픔과 공포 속에서 아이는 영문을 모른 채 죽어간다. 어떤 불순물도 섞이지 않은 순수한 원한이다. 그렇게 얻은 아이의 손가락을 명주천에 싸서 보관한다. 꾸덕꾸덕 마를 즈음 그것을 젖물이 흐르는 가슴에 두르고 백 일을 지낸다. 그렇게 아이를 얼러서 자신의 용도대로 원혼을 부리려는 것이다.

이렇게 만들어 가진 그 유골을 명두(明斗)라 하기 때문에 그녀의 별명이 명두집이 된 것이었다. 그녀의 영험이 남달랐던 것은 그런 명두를 세 개씩이나 품고 있기 때문이라고 했다. 간장이나 된장독 말고 그녀의 집

children. A newborn doesn't die from starvation right away. It isn't until the third or fourth day when the baby starts crying uncontrollably, flailing its arms and legs. That's when she shoves the baby in a dark earthenware jar and covers it with a heavy earthenware lid. Hungry, cold, and alone in the dark jar, the baby senses death is near. After a day or two in those conditions, even the newest of newborns musters all its might to throw off the lid. She weighs the lid down with a large rock. The horror felt by the child, having no prior exposure to the world, is as pure as can be. Eventually, even the lid, weighed down by the rock, begins to budge. She sharpens a knife and waits to chop off one of the baby's fingers when it sticks out from under the lid. One fell swoop does it. The child rolls back into the darkness of the jar, crying hysterically. A few more heavy rocks. The child dies in pain and fear, completely oblivious to all else. The child's agony is of the purest variety, free of any impurities. She wraps the baby's finger in silk and waits until it dries stiff. She then binds it around her chest, which still drips with breast milk, and keeps it there for one hundred days. And so she used the babies to serve her own purposes.

에 과연 아이의 시체를 담아둔 옹기가 따로 있는지 사람들이 확인할 길은 없었으나, 그녀의 방 보꾹 한 켠에 보시기만한 백자 항아리가 신주단지처럼 모셔져 있다는 것만은 사실이었다. 그 안에 세 아이의 손가락이 들어 있을 거라고 했다. 이리하여 사람들은 명두집이, 목숨 말고는 아무것도 훼손되지 않은 아이들의 시신을 내 발치에 묻었다는 사실을 몰랐다. 어째서 하루도 빠짐없이 나에게 다녀갔는지도 그들은 당연히 알지 못했다.

그녀의 명두의 효험으로 마을의 병든 자들을 치료하고 다스릴 동안, 산 너머 곽 초시네로 보내졌던 딸은 그 집 행랑아범과 혼인하여 아들딸을 각각 둘씩이나 낳았다. 종살이나 다름없이 살면서도 네 자식을 온전히 건사하며 텔레비전과 냉장고까지 장만할 수 있었던 것은, 억척도 억척이지만 흐르는 세월이 그럭저럭 사람을 먹고살게 했기 때문이었다. 아들아이는 아비가 뱀에 물려 죽은 뒤로 마을을 떠나 타지를 떠돌았으나, 역시 세월 따라 고을이 읍이 되고 읍이 대처가 되면서 그럭저럭 입에 풀칠은 하고 살았다. 모천을 떠난 물고기처럼, 둥지를 떠난 뜸부기처럼, 위태위태 세월의 파고를 넘으면

Any dead body part attained for such reasons was called a *myeongdu*, a relic shamans used to call on their patron saints. That's why people called her the Myeongdu Lady. Her powers were particularly strong because she had three of them, supposedly. The villagers had no way of verifying that the large clay jars in her yard for soy sauce and soybean paste didn't contain infant corpses. It was true, though, that she had ceremoniously placed a white porcelain jar on a shelf under the wooden beam that ran across the exposed ceiling in her room. People claimed that the jar housed three fingers, each belonging to a different child. No one knew she had buried her babies, all of them unharmed except for what was done to their short lives. Of course, they didn't know why she came to visit me every single day.

While she healed sick villagers with the powers granted her by the *myeongdu* in her possession, the daughter she gave away to the Kwak family over the mountain married their manservant. Together, they had two sons and two daughters. Though they lived as servants, they were able to raise their own four children and even purchase a television and refrigerator for their home. They worked hard to

서 어떻게든 목숨을 부지해 갔으므로 아이들에 대한 그녀의 시름은 더 이상 지속되지 않았다.

뒷골도 많이 변했다. 전기가 들어오고 전화가 설치됐다. 간이 상수도 시설이 생기면서 샘은 개구리들의 차지가 되었다. 버스가 오가고 멀지 않은 곳에 보건소도 들어섰다. 버스를 타고 나가면 현대식 병원에 갈 수도 있었다. 이제 더는 굶어 죽거나 버려지는 아이와 노인이 생기지 않았다. 그러나 명두집을 찾아오는 병자들은 줄지 않았다. 인근의 보건소나 병원보다 명두집을 더 많이 찾았다. 날이 갈수록 그녀의 낯빛은 벚꽃잎처럼 허여멀겋게 피어올랐고 턱밑 주름이 세 겹으로 늘어났다. 이마가 넓어지고 광대뼈가 묻히면서 원만무애대비심대덕보살처럼 되어갔다. 눈빛은 태평하고 풍채는 당당하여 그녀를 보기만 해도 잡귀가 줄행랑을 칠 것 같았다. 산처럼 늠름하게 버티고 앉은 그녀는, 맥이 막혀 흑빛으로 찾아오는 사람들을 향해 불망! 이라고 포함을 질렀다. 기함을 하며 하얗게 질리는 병자들에게 잊은 게 있지? 라고 연이어 물었다. 잊은 게 있어. 그게 너를 살린 건지도 모르고.

get where they were, but time also played a large part. The Myeongdu Lady's son left the village after his father died. As a country village—with time— becomes a town and a town becomes a commercial center, he, too, with time, managed to get by somewhat decently. Like fish that leave their streams for larger waters, like waterrails that leave their nests, her children managed to survive the fierce waves of time. She didn't have to wrestle with what she had done to them anymore.

The old village also changed. Power lines went up and telephones were installed. When small-scale waterworks facilities came in, frogs took over the abandoned stream. Buses came and went, and a health clinic opened its doors not too far away. A bus ride out of the village took you to a modern hospital. No more babies or older folk were abandoned and no more died of starvation. Yet the sick flocked to the Myeongdu Lady. More went to her than the clinic or hospital. As the days went by, her face bloomed like a murky-white cherry blossom and she grew three chins. She resembled Buddha more and more as her forehead widened and her cheekbones sunk. Her eyes were serene but her figure was imposing. Any of the frivolous demons

길을 뚫기 위해 산자락이 뭉텅 잘려나가고 마침내 나와 내 곁의 많은 나무들이 몽땅 베어질 위기에 처했을 때도 명두집은 냅다 소리를 질렀었다. 자신의 키보다 대여섯 배나 큰 나를 등에 업고 인질범처럼 설쳤다. 너희가 뭣 땜에 지금까지 살아왔는데? 누가 늬들을 살렸는데? 무엇이 너희들을 살게 했는지 벌써 잊어? 아직 몰라? 끝없이 이어지는 의문형 외침 때문에, 그녀와 대치하고 있던 공사 관계자와 마을 사람들은 뭔가 대답을 해야 하는 거 아닌가 싶어 서로의 얼굴을 멋쩍게 바라보았다. 길목길목에 버티고 서서 아리송한 질문을 던지고 5초 안에 대답할 것을 요구하는 탈출 게임의 도깨비 탈 보조 진행자를 바라보듯 사람들은 명두집을 건너다보았다. 우리를 살린 것이 저 나무인가? 자연을 말하는 건가? 숲이 우리를 살리는 거라고 말하는 건지도 몰라. 저 여자는 분명 자연보호 운동가야, 그렇지 않아? 당치도 않은 말들이 사람들 사이에서 오갔다. 사람들은 저마다 나무와 숲이 자신들을 어떻게 살렸는지를 생각했다. 먹을 것이 없어 죽어갈 때 열매와 뿌리를 나누어주

were sure to run away at the sight of her. She sat in her room like a stately mountain and shouted ruthlessly at her visitors, whose countenances were black.

"Don't forget!" It frightened them and they turned faint and pale. "You've forgotten, haven't you? You've forgotten! It's what saved you, and you don't even know it!"

To make the road leading into the village, they carved out a huge chunk of the mountain at its base. When they were about to chop us all down, the Myeongdu Lady continued with her shouting. She took me hostage and refused to let down—it didn't matter that I was five, six times bigger than her.

"Don't you know why you're still here today? Who do you think kept you alive? Have you forgotten what's kept you alive? You still don't realize?"

Baffled by her endless interrogations, the construction crew and villagers simply exchanged uncomfortable glances. It was as though she had become the host of some sort of escape game show, guarding the street corners and demanding an-

던 숲, 겨울 땔감을 주어 얼어 죽지 않게 했던 숲, 물을 주고 목재를 주었던 숲, 짝을 만날 수 있도록 은밀한 그늘을 드리우고, 용을 쓰는 남정네의 파정에 맞추어 신음을 내지를 때 적당히 가려주고 얼버무려주던 풀밭과 바람과 이파리들……. 그러나 그런 숲들은 산을 가득 덮을 만큼 기세등등하게 남아 있었다. 그리고 더 이상은 숲에서 열매를 따지 않았으며 땔감을 얻지 않았으며 우발적 정사를 치르지도 않았다. 사람들은 고개를 끄덕이다가도 도리질을 쳤다.

명두집 하나 끌어내는 건 일도 아니었다. 근육질의 많은 인부들과 중장비는 대군을 무찌르고도 남을 만했다. 그런데도 결국 그들은 아녀자 하나를 저지하지 못했고, 경찰 간부와 도지사도 한숨만 쉬며 고개를 가로저었다. 까짓거 방향을 쪼매만 틀죠 뭐. 눈치를 챈 현장소장이 비굴하게 말했을 때 이의를 다는 사람은 아무도 없었다.

그들은 반년 전의 놀라웠던 사태를 기억하는 것 같았다. 산 아래에서 터진 전쟁이 막바지에 이르고 있었다. 그동안 고단하고 궁핍한 삶을 이어왔던 산 밑 판자촌이

swers to bewildering questions in just five seconds time. One could hear nonsensical responses debated amongst them.

"Is it that tree that saved us?"

"Is she talking about nature?"

"Maybe she's trying to say that the forest is what's kept us alive."

"I bet she's an environmental activist."

In the meantime, she burned her bridges and tied herself to me. The others got to thinking about how the trees in the forest had preserved their lives. When they were dying of hunger, the forest had given them plants and roots to eat. Its firewood had kept them from freezing to death in the winter. It had given them water and lumber. It had provided shade for clandestine encounters; the grassy beds, the breeze, and the leaves muffled the woman's moans in tune with the man's rhythms. Now, forests like that proudly blanketed the mountains. No longer did people go there to find food, collect firewood, or make love spontaneously. They nodded their heads in concession, but shook them soon after.

Dragging the Myeongdu Lady away wasn't what was hard; the brawny laborers and heavy equip-

포클레인으로 짓이겨졌다. 빈촌을 정리하고 산중턱에 새로운 주거단지를 개발한다고 했다. 집다운 집이 한 채도 없었으므로 부수고 말 것도 없었다. 중장비가 탱크처럼 지나갔다. 철거반원들은 한가한 보병처럼 중장비 뒤를 따랐다. 그들이 지나가기만 하면 저절로 폐허가 되었다. 승산 없는 싸움이었다. 주인이 따로 있던 땅이었다. 나가라면 나갈 수밖에 없었다. 갈 곳 없는 사람들은 천막을 치고 뭉쳐 대응했으며, 나중에는 마을 한가운데다 높다란 탑을 쌓고 그 위에 올라가 투신을 무기로 마지막 저항에 나섰다. 그런 일에는 으레 내분이 있게 마련이었다. 저항에 지친 자들이 하나둘 저들의 회유에 넘어가기 시작했다. 당초의 보상 요구를 반으로 접고 투항하는 사람이 늘어났다. 마을에는 높다란 투쟁철탑이 을씨년스럽게 서 있었다. 마지막까지 버티던 청년이 홧김에 유일한 승강용 사다리를 부숴버리고 스스로 그 안에 갇혔다. 쓰러진 기둥 하나가 계곡을 가로질러 위태롭게 뻗어 있을 뿐이었다. 아무도 그곳에 오를 수 없었고, 그곳의 청년도 내려올 수 없었다. 밑에서 쏘아대는 로프는 매번 중간에도 닿지 못한 채 푸르르 흘

ment could take on a large army. But in the end, they lost to a woman. Even the police chiefs and provincial governor could do nothing but sigh and shake their heads. The site manager gave in and said, "So we'll redirect the road a little. No big deal." No one raised any objections whatsoever.

They seemed to remember what had happened half a year ago. The war that broke out beneath the mountain was nearing its final stages. Poclain excavators had crushed the weary, destitute shantytown. They were planning to wipe out the village and build a new residential complex on the mountainside. No house was worth salvaging. The heavy machinery drove by like tanks. The demolition crew marched behind the machines like foot soldiers. They left destruction wherever they passed. It was a losing battle. The land had an owner. When told to leave, they had to move out. Those with nowhere to go pitched tents and refused to leave. As a final show of resistance, they erected a tower in the middle of the village and threatened to jump off its highest platform.

But movements of this nature are always bound to splinter. Eventually, those who grew tired of resisting started to give in to the conciliatory offers.

러내렸다. 3주가 지나도록 청년은 내려오지 않았다. 그의 생사를 아무도 알 수 없었다.

그때 홀연히 나섰던 사람이 명두집이었다. 나이로 보나 몸집으로 보나 나설 사람이 아니었다. 폭이 너무 좁은 데다 높기만 너무 높아 전문 인명 구조반원들도 계곡에 가로로 뻗어 있는 철제 빔을 바라만 보고 있었다. 명두집이 로프 한쪽 끝을 잡고 그 빔 위에 올라섰다. 그녀의 통통한 몸이 작고 검은 새처럼 보일 만큼 아득했다. 그녀가 떨어질까 봐 사람들은 숨조차 크게 쉬지 못하고 고개를 젖힌 채 입을 벌리고 있었다. 경악하는 사람들을 아랑곳 않고 명두집은 느리고 안정된 걸음을 천천히 옮겼다. 구조반원들이 타고 오를 수 있도록 로프 끝을 꼭대기 기둥에 단단히 맨 그녀는, 다시 공중 줄타기 묘기를 부리듯 좁고 아득한 철제 빔 위를 걸어 유유히 지상으로 내려왔다. 청년은 그 위에서 탈진해 쓰러져 있었다.

나이에 어울리지 않는 기적 같은 균형감각을, 사람들은 직접 눈으로 보았으면서도 믿지 못했다. 그녀의 기적은 급히 연락을 받고 달려온 방송 기자에 의해 촬영

One after the other, the villagers surrendered, halving the amount of money they'd first demanded in compensation. The tall steel tower stood against the dreary village sky. In his rage, the last young man on the platform broke the ladder hoist, trapping himself. A single, fallen beam stretched out dangerously across the valley. No one could get up there, and there was no way he could get down. The ropes they tried to throw to him couldn't make it even halfway up before falling limply back down. For three weeks he didn't come down. No one knew whether he was dead or alive.

Out of the blue, the Myeongdu Lady stepped into the picture. Judging from her age and size, she wasn't the right person for the job. So narrow and so high up was the steel beam that stretched out over the valley that even the trained rescue crew just stood there. The Myeongdu Lady grabbed one end of the rope and climbed the pillar. Her tiny, round body looked like a small blackbird in the distance. The crowd watched with necks jerked back and mouths agape, holding their breath in case she fell. Unfazed by the astonished onlookers, she walked slowly and stably. She tied the rope securely to the top of the pillar for the rescuers to

되었고 여섯 차례에 걸쳐 전국에 방영됐다. 기자의 질문에 그녀는 짧게 두 마디로 대답했을 뿐이다. 어떻게 그럴 수가? 나는 죽음이 두렵지 않아요. 비결이 있다면? 잊지 않으니까……

그때도 그녀는 잊지 않는다는 말을 했고, 그렇게 말하는 명두집의 눈빛과 서슬은 이승의 것 같지 않아 곁에 있는 사람들이 모두 덜덜 떨었다. 그러니까 나를 베어내지 못하고 결국 도로의 진행 방향을 약간 틀 수밖에 없었던 것은 나무가 중요해서도, 명두집이 원하는 대답의 타당성 때문도, 그녀를 끌어낼 인력과 방법이 없었기 때문도 아니었다. 서슬. 묵살했다가는 이승은 물론 저승에서마저 반드시 급살귀신이 되게 할 것 같은 그녀의 무시무시한 서슬 때문이었다.

내가 네 통의 가루후추와 두 병의 제초제로 숨이 끊어졌을 때도 그랬다. 이제 죽었으니 나무를 포기하겠거니 여겼던 사람들은 그녀의 여전한 포함과 발악에 두 손을 들고 혀를 내둘렀다. 그녀를 말릴 수 있는 사람은 아무도 없었다.

그녀의 남편이 뱀에 물려 죽고, 나라가 온통 전쟁에

climb up. Then, with the ease of a tightrope walker, she walked back across the narrow beam and made her way down to land. She said the young man had fainted from exhaustion.

Though they witnessed the scene with their own eyes, they found it hard to believe that a person of that age could have such perfect balance. A TV reporter had captured the miraculous feat on film after rushing to the scene. It aired nationwide six times. When the reporter attempted an interview, she gave two responses and no more.

"How'd you do it?"

"I'm not afraid of death."

"What's your secret?"

"I don't forget."

The onlookers trembled when she said those words, for both the look in her eyes and the menace in her aura were hard to characterize as human. It was this presence about her that kept them from cutting me down, leaving them with no other choice but to slightly alter the road's layout. It wasn't because trees were important, nor because the Myeongdu Lady's questions were reasonable, and certainly not because they lacked the manpower or means to drag her away. Her terrible aura threat-

휩쓸리고, 마을 남정네들이 돌아가며 그녀를 욕보일 때까지만 해도 그녀는 벙어리 반편이처럼 말없이 당하기만 했었다. 넋이 나간 사람이었으며 퀭하게 열린 눈은 이승을 보고 있지 않았다.

그녀의 남편은 독도 없는 떼뱀에게 물려 죽었다. 더덕밭으로 가는 길엔 이슬에 젖은 여뀌들로 무성했다. 여뀌밭을 통과해야 했으나 그곳은 누룩뱀들의 천지였다. 누룩뱀들이 더덕을 지키는 꼴이어서 손을 타지 않은 더덕들은 무만한 뿌리를 내리고 방자하게 향기를 뿜고 있었다. 모르지는 않았으나 더덕 욕심에 눈멀어 여뀌밭으로 들어선 그녀의 남편은 한창 교미 중이던 떼뱀에게 다리를 휘감겨 넘어졌고, 바닥의 돌멩이에 부딪쳐 이마를 크게 다쳤다. 화가 난 그는 장작을 있는 대로 날라다 쌓고 여뀌밭을 몽땅 불태워 버렸다. 더덕을 흡족하게 얻었던 그는 다음 해에도 그곳을 아무 생각 없이 지나다가 떼뱀에게 걸려 목숨을 잃었다. 여뀌는 어느새 전해보다 더 무성하게 자라 있었고 뱀의 숫자도 결코 줄어들지 않았던 것이다. 온몸을 물렸으나 뱀독으로 죽은 게 아니었다. 놀라 기절을 한 그의 목과 가슴을 뱀들이

ened to turn anyone who went against her wishes into a sinister phantom in this life and the next life.

Thanks to her, they couldn't do anything to me after I died from the four containers of pepper powder and two bottles of weed killer. Surely she would forfeit the tree now that it was dead, they figured. When she shouted at the top of her lungs, however, commanding the spirits she believed to be inside them, they threw their hands into the air and could find no words. No one could beat her.

She hadn't always been like this. After her husband died by snakes and war had ravaged the entire country, the menfolk in the village had taken turns disgracing her. She hadn't said a word and had borne all of it like a mute fool. Her soul had gone; her hollow eyes were not on this world.

The rat snakes that had killed her husband were non-venomous. On the way to the patch of prized *deodeok* (bonnet bellflower roots) there was a field of overgrown water peppers wet with dew. One had to pass through it to get to the rarer plants. Only, it teemed with rat snakes. The rat snakes guarded the *deodeok*, whose roots were as big as white radishes, and seemed impudent, making no effort to hide their scent. Fixed on getting his hands on some, he

대나무 뿌리처럼 휘감아 숨통을 끊어놓은 거였다. 죽은 그의 시체는 참혹했다. 뱀들은 그의 두 눈을 파고들었으며 입과 귀와 콧구멍과 똥구멍에도 뱀의 몸통이 득시글거리며 박혀 있었다. 몽땅 타버렸던 여뀌밭은 다시 생명의 열기를 뿜으며 번져갔고, 뱀들은 그 안에서 여전히 교미를 하며 번득였고, 더덕도 통통하게 다시 살이 쪘다.

그 여뀌밭은 전쟁이 터져 마을 뒷산이 반나마 불길에 휩싸였을 때 다시 탔다. 산으로 도망쳤던 사람들과, 총살당해 버려진 사람들과, 손을 묶여 끌려가던 사람들이 그 여뀌밭과 소나무와 상수리나무와 오리나무와 함께 재가 되었다. 군인들은 염소와 돼지를 모조리 잡아먹고 소를 훔쳤으며 개를 끌고 갔다. 산과 마을은 황폐하여 생명이 살 수 없는 곳이 되었으나 시나브로 다시 여뀌가 자라고 나무들이 새순을 틔우면서 끔찍한 기억들을 푸르게 뒤덮어 버렸다. 새끼 염소가 울고 개가 짖고 다시 시냇물이 흘렀다.

겨우 목숨을 건진 사내들이 처음 기운을 내어 한 짓이란 홀로 남은 명두집을 겁간하는 일이었다. 서리꾼처

found himself in the water pepper patch. The rat snakes were at the height of their mating activities, and the Myeongdu Lady's husband had lost his balance when one of them wrapped itself around his ankle. He fell on his face, injuring his forehead badly. When he'd gotten back up, furious, he gathered all the firewood in sight and burned the entire field down. Now he could pick *deodeok* to his heart's content. He returned a year later thinking things would be fine—but the snakes had returned. The water peppers had grown thicker than before, and the snakes were certainly no fewer in number. They bit him all over his body, but in the end even that wasn't what killed him. He'd blacked out from the shock and the snakes had wrapped themselves around his neck and chest, suffocating him to death. His corpse was grotesque. The snakes had burrowed into his eye sockets. They swarmed in and out of his mouth, ears, nostrils, and even his anus. The water pepper field that had been burned down flourished again with new life, the snakes flashed their gleaming scales and mated as they used to, and the *deodeok* grew plump once more.

The field burned down again when war broke out and fire claimed more than half of the moun-

럼 은밀히 찾아와 타고 누르거나, 헛간 검불 속으로 끌고 가거나, 나물 뜯는 거친 풀밭에 엎어뜨리거나, 산길에 숨어 있다가 갈고리 같은 손으로 그녀를 나꿔챘다. 겉으론 입을 모아 불쌍하다며 혀를 차던 자들이 혼자가 되거나 밤이 되면 눈 귀 없고 양심도 없는 귀두(龜頭) 몽둥이로 돌변하여 그녀를 을러댔다. 명두집이 세 번째로 묻은 시신은 그렇게 생긴 아이였고, 그 마지막 아이를 묻은 뒤로 그녀는 갑자기 달라졌다.

그녀에게 가장 못되게 굴었던 세근이라는 사내가 어느 날 저녁 그녀의 부름을 받았다. 호롱불 밑에서 왕골 맷방석을 매고 있던 그는 밖의 인기척에 손을 멈추었다. 아무 소리도 들리지 않았다. 다시 왕골 줄기를 부여잡으려 하자 어떤 기미가 다시 느껴졌다. 조심스레 문을 열었다. 어둠이 내린 마당 한가운데에 그녀가 장승처럼 우뚝 서 있었다. 질겁을 했으나 못된 짓이라면 침을 흘리고 나서는 그답게 곧장 회심의 미소를 지으며 중얼거렸다. 이제 길이 나서 내 맛을 제대로 아는 모양이지. 명두집은 말없이 돌아섰다. 세근은 매던 맷방석을 팽개치고 그녀의 뒤를 따랐다.

tain behind the village. Everything became ash—the villagers who'd fled to the hills, the discarded dead, and the people who'd been dragged into the fields with their hands tied. They were engulfed along with the water pepper field and the pine trees and the oak trees and the alder trees. The soldiers killed the last of the goats and pigs to feed themselves. They stole the cows and dragged the dogs away with them. The mountain and the village were left in ruins and could no longer support life. Slowly but surely, however, the water peppers returned and new shoots began to bud on the trees. The greenery grew over every painful memory still there. The young goats bleated, the dogs barked, and the stream flowed once again.

After the first terrible shock of war subsided and the surviving men learned to live with it, they set out to rape the widowed Myeongdu Lady. Like thieves in the night, they approached her silently before lunging at her. Some dragged her to the piles of straw while others threw her down on the field of tall grass or hid in the mountains and snatched her, their arms hooked, when she passed by. In public, they had pity on her, but the loneliness of the night turned them into something else,

집 마당에 도착한 그녀는 남편이 죽은 뒤로 줄곧 닫고 살았던 입을 처음으로 뗐다. 좀 도와주셔야겠는데요. 그러곤 헛간으로 갔다. 세근은 호기롭게 중얼거리며 그녀를 따랐다. 어려울 것 없지, 암.

헛간에는 커다란 남자가 널브러져 있었다. 어둠 속에서 보아도 그건 시체였다. 구름이 걷히면서 무너진 헛간 지붕을 뚫고 퍼런 달빛이 쏟아져 내렸다. 죽은 사내의 몸 여기저기에는 깊고 처참한 상처가 나 있었다. 이미 심장이 멎은 상태여서 피는 더 이상 흐르지 않았다. 피떡을 머금은 상처들이 활짝 입을 벌리고 있을 뿐이었다. 달빛을 받아 그것들은 흑단처럼 검게 번들거렸다. 세근은 헛간 한 켠에 얼어붙듯 서 있었다. 서 있지만 말고 좀……. 그녀가 시신의 머리를 감싸 들며 심상하게 말했다. 그동안 성가셨던 구유를 옮기기라도 하는 것처럼 태평했다. 세근은 가까스로 시체의 두 발을 움켜잡았다. 드는 순간 아직 경직되지 않은 시체가 출렁거렸다. 세근은 엉덩방아를 찧으며 나동그라졌다. 그런 주검들이 심심찮게 발견되던 때였다. 나중에 밝혀진 거지만 명두집 헛간에서 시신으로 발견된 자는 1년 넘게 토

hardened, seething desire unable to see or hear, let alone distinguish right from wrong. The third baby she buried was conceived this way, and she would never be the same.

One night, she went to the house of Saegeun, the man who had treated her the worst. A kerosene lamp flickered. He was weaving dried sedge grasses to make a mat when he sensed someone was outside. His hands froze. He heard nothing. He was about to pick up the stem he dropped when he sensed it again. Cautiously, he opened the door. She stood like a wooden guardian post in the middle of the yard where darkness had fallen. He was frightened at first, but then a smile spread across his face—he was the type to drool at the thought of a dirty deed. He was certain that she had come back for more. The Myeongdu Lady turned around without a word. Saegeun left the unfinished mat as it was and followed her.

Upon arriving at her front yard, she spoke for the first time since her husband had died.

"I'm afraid I need your help."

She headed for the shed.

"Not a problem," he muttered to himself.

He salivated as he followed.

벌대가 찾던 마지막 공산 유격대장이었다.

명두집은 시신을 성황당 언덕까지 혼자 옮기다시피했다. 가끔씩 힘든 허리를 펴며 세근을 한심하다는 듯노려볼 뿐이었다. 세근은 그때 명두집의 심상찮은 눈빛을 보았다. 행동은 굼뜨고 나른해 보이기까지 했지만커다란 남자 시체를 옮기는 그녀에게서는 놀라운 힘이느껴졌다. 그것은 힘이라기보단 일종의 기세 같은 것이었다. 몸이 아니라 눈빛과 서슬에서 뿜어져 나왔다. 천지를 뒤덮은 밤의 수꿀스런 기운도 그녀를 어쩌지 못했다. 아무도 당해내지 못할 그녀의 완강하고 무섭고 당찬 기품을 세근은 이미 그 밤에 보았다. 성황당 돌무더기로 시신을 수습하고 난 그녀는 우두커니 서 있던 세근의 어깨를 떠밀었다. 산이 덮쳐오는 것만큼이나 센그녀의 손길에 밀려 나자빠지며 세근은 오줌을 쌌다. 그 뒤로 세근은 그녀 곁에 얼씬도 못 했고, 다른 사내들도 그녀를 엄두조차 내지 못했다. 철거 반대 탑을 오르던 명두집의 기적과, 살았을 때나 죽었을 때나 나를 지켜냈던 무시무시한 서슬은 사실 그때부터 싹트고 있었던 것이다.

A good-sized man lay sprawled out in the shed.
It was a corpse—unmistakable even in the dark. As
the clouds cleared, the blue moonlight streamed in
from the broken roof. Deep, grotesque wounds
covered the dead body. The wounds gaped open
and had filled with blood, which no longer flowed
after the heart had stopped beating. The blood
shone like ebony in the moonlight. Saegeun stood
frozen in a corner of the shed.

"Don't just stand there."

She lifted the head as she spoke. She went about
it so easily; she would've gotten rid of an old
trough the same way. Saegeun pulled himself together and took hold of both ankles. As soon as
they lifted both ends, the corpse sagged and Saegeun fell back, landing hard on his rear. It wasn't
uncommon to find corpses like that around that
time. It was later revealed that the body found in
the Myeongdu Lady's shed had been a runaway
Communist guerilla commander, pursued by a pu-
nitive expedition force for over a year.

The Myeongdu Lady practically dragged the
corpse to the hill behind the village shrine herself.
She paused from time to time to straighten her
aching back and to roll her eyes at Saegeun. He

세근이라는 사내는 간이 돌처럼 굳는 바람에 부황이나 죽어버렸다. 더 이상 굶어 죽는 사람은 없었지만 누구는 늙어 죽고 누구는 놀라 죽고 누구는 홧병이 나 죽었다. 사람들이 허리앓이 무릎앓이 배앓이 가슴앓이 속병으로 고생하는 동안 명두집은 허옇게 살이 찌고 목소리가 굵게 늘어지며 영험이 깊어졌다. 표정이 있는 듯 없는 듯 화엄성중 탱화 속 인물처럼 근엄한 낯빛으로 사람에게 붙은 귀신을 쫓아내어 병을 다스렸다. 나무 방망이로 다듬잇돌을 두드리고 복화술로 어린 영혼의 음성을 흉내 냈다. 문밖에서 그 소리를 듣고 있자면 어린 영혼의 소리는 멀리서 새가 지저귀는 것 같았고 나무 방망이 소리는 목탁음 같았다. 그녀를 찾는 사람들은 대부분 여자들이었다. 병원엘 가도 소용이 없고 시름시름 앓기만 하던 사람들이 마침내 그녀의 다듬잇돌 앞에 기어와 코를 박고 엎어졌다. 귀신이 붙었다거나 귀신을 쫓는다는 말을 그녀는 자신의 입으로 하지 않았다. 잊은 게 있지? 라고 물을 뿐이었다. 그녀의 말을 병자들은 얼른 알아듣지 못했다. 그녀가 땀을 흘리며 다듬잇돌을 한나절이나 두들기고, 어린 영혼을 불러오고,

sensed something solemn about the look in her eyes. She may have moved slowly, but it took great strength for a woman to haul a large male cadaver. It couldn't have been mere strength. It was a force. It radiated from her eyes, from her very demeanor. Not even the shudder-inducingvibes of night when it blankets the universe had a hold on her. That night, Saegeun saw her tenacity, the terrifying force that no one would be able to face. After dealing with the corpse at the stone heap behind the shrine, she charged at Saegeun, who had just been standing there, aiming for his shoulders. It was like a mountain had slammed into him. It knocked him down and he found his pants were wet. From that day forward, he never appeared before her again, and no one else took their chances. It was then that the power behind her miraculous feat on the beam and the intimidation with which she guarded me before and after my death had formed.

Saegeun's liver hardened into a rock and edema eventually killed him. No one starved to death anymore, but someone died of old age, another from shock, and another in a sudden, violent bout of rage. They suffered from back pains, knee pains,

허텅지거리와 욕지거리를 섞어 야단을 치며 호달구고 나서야 그녀를 찾은 사람들은 뭘 잊었었는지 자신들의 멀고 깊은 기억 속에서 간신히 건져 올렸다.

죽거나 죽인 아이를 떠올렸다. 죽거나 죽인 부모를 떠올렸다. 더러는 임진왜란이나 병자호란 때 죽은 조상을 떠올리기도 했다.

먼저 보낸 아이를 잊었어요.

왜 보냈나?

그녀는 되물었다.

……살려고요. 명두님도 아시잖아요, 내가 살려고요. 그땐 다 그랬잖아요.

그래서 살았군.

그랬겠죠.

그런데 어째서 잊었나?

잊고 싶었겠죠. 잊어야 하는 거 아닌가요?

그런 대화가 다듬잇돌 방망이 소리와 새소리 사이로 끝없이 이어졌다.

명두집은 도리질을 쳤다.

살자고 애들을 죽였으니, 잘 살아남는 게 죽은 애들에

chest pains, and all manner of internal diseases. In contrast, the Myeongdu Lady grew plump, her voice thickened, and her spiritual powers deepened. The somber look in her face was reminiscent of the Guardians of the Buddhist Creed painted behind the altar at the temple. She cast out spirits and healed infirmities. She beat on a fulling block with two mallets as she mimicked the voices of young souls. If you stood outside her doors, you heard what sounded like birds chirping and monks striking their wooden *moktak*. Mostly women came to see the Myeongdu Lady. When nothing else could alleviate their pain—they'd already seen all the doctors—they dragged themselves to the Myeongdu Lady and fell flat on their noses in front of her fulling block. She spoke to them as they reeled in pain, but she never mentioned any evil spirits.

"You've forgotten, haven't you?" That's the first thing she asked. They didn't catch on right away. It took a day's work of pounding vigorously on the fulling block, calling on young souls, and shouting at her patients—sometimes nonsense, sometimes obscenities—before they finally delved deep enough into their memories to recall what they had long forgotten.

대한 도리겠구먼.

병든 아낙들은 눈물을 흘리며 고개를 끄덕였다.

그런데 어쩌자고 병이 들고 지랄이야!

아낙들은 콧물까지 흘렸다.

죽은 사람에 대한 도리로 잘 살려면 어떻게 해야 하는 줄 알아?

그제야 아낙들은 고개를 들어 명두집을 바라보았다. 그 면상에다 대고 명두집은 냅다 소리를 내질렀다.

불망!

그 소리는 경천동지할 만큼 커서 대부분의 아낙들은 뒤로 나가자빠졌다.

내가 병들어 죽을 거였으면 어쩌자고 애먼 애들을 죽였나? 내가 살려고 애들을 죽였으면 미안해서라도 살아남아야지.

병 털고 살아남으려고 이렇게 명두님을 찾았잖아요.

죽지 않으려면 죽는 걸 겁내선 안 돼. 죽는 걸 겁내니까 지랄 염병 속병이 생기지. 겁내지 않으려면 도망치거나 잊지 말고 그놈과 평생 함께 살아야 돼. 도망치거나 잊어뿌리면 겁이 들어오게 되고, 미쳐 죽거나 뺴들

They remembered their dead children—the ones they had killed and the ones that had died on their own. They remembered dead parents. Some remembered ancestors that died during the Imjin War or the second Manchu invasion.

"I let my child go before me."

"Why did you let her go?"

"I needed to live. Mrs. Myeongdu, you understand, don't you? I needed to live. We all did back then."

"So that's how you stayed alive."

"I suppose so."

"How could you forget?"

"I wanted to forget. Aren't you supposed to forget such things?"

These conversations extended between the beating of the mallets on the fulling block and the chirping of birds.

The Myeongdu Lady shook her head.

"If you killed your children in order to live, the least you can do for them is to live the best life you can. Am I right?"

The sick village women nodded, tears streaming down their face.

"Then what're you doing? Falling ill like this,

빼들 말라 죽어. 알어? 잊는 게 죽는 거라구. 그러면 이 년아, 애를 죽인 게 무슨 소용이야? 니가 죽는 순간 애도 진짜로 죽어버린다는 걸 알아야 해. 니가 죽지 않아야 구천의 애도 억울하지 않을 거 아냐. 알아먹어? 니가 살려고 애들을 죽였으면 어떻게든 잘 살아야지. 병 걸리지 말고 미치지 않고 빼들빼들 말라 죽지 않으려면 죽는 걸 겁내지 말아야 하고, 죽는 걸 겁내지 않으려면 죽음과 잘 사귀어야 하는 거야. 죽음이 사람을 살리는 이치를 알아야 해. 죽은 애들이 너를 살렸듯이, 니가 살아야 걔들 죽음이 헛되지 않게 되는 거잖아. 헛되지 않으면 걔들은 살아 있는 거야. 걔들을 잊어버리면 슬슬 죽는 게 겁나고 도망치고 싶고, 그러다 보면 니가 병들어 죽어서 애도 죽는 거야. 피하지 말고 사귀어야 돼. 삼켜서 몸 안에 고이, 길이길이 간직해. 잊지 말라니까. 불망!

소리를 질러대도 얼른 알아듣지 못하기는 마찬가지였다.

어떡하면 잊지 않을까요?

시키는 대로 할 텨?

turning into thismess!"

Their noses ran, too.

"Do you want me to tell you how to honor the dead with your life?"

That's when the women would lift their heads and look intently at the Myeongdu Lady. She screamed full in their faces:

"Do not forget!"

The earth-shattering howl of the Myeongdu Lady knocked over most of the women.

"If you're going to end up dying this way, what was the point in killing those blameless children? You killed 'em to spare your own life! The least you can do is not die!"

"That's why I'm here, Mrs. Myeongdu. I want to be healed."

"If you don't wanna die, you can't be scared of dying. Shit, that's why you're all getting sick left and right! If you don't wanna be frightened anymore, don't run away: Don't forget.

"Stay with your man for the rest of your life. Fear creeps in when you run away or forget. You either die mad or you wither within yourself. You hear me? When you forget, you die! Your babe's death is meaningless! What you don't know is that the

하고말고요.

명두집은 보꾹 한 켠에 모셔진 보시기만한 백자 항아리를 가리켰다.

저기다 절을 해. 아홉 번을 해.

그러곤 말했다.

문지방이 닳도록 와서 절을 해야겠지만 니년들이 그럴 리는 만무하고, 대신 배냇저고리 남아 있는 게 있거나 떨어진 배꼽 보관하고 있는 거 있으면 가져와. 다 가져올 필요는 없고 조금만 떼 와. 그러면 그걸 내가 삼켜서 이 몸속에다 간직할 테니게. 그리구 내가 죽기 전까지는 내둥 돌아다닐 거니까 나를 보면 걸어다니는 사자 보드끼 맘속으로 아홉 번 절을 하고 식구처럼 반겨. 도망치지 말고. 알겠어?

명두집의 분부대로 아낙들은 배냇저고리의 한 귀퉁이를 오리거나 마른 태반 한쪽을 떼어다 그녀에게 바쳤다. 그도 저도 없는 사람들은 아이가 뻈던 베개의 일부를, 아니면 아이가 묻힌 땅의 흙 한 자밤이라도 갖다 바쳤다. 초하루와 보름날은 일부러 시간을 내어 명두집에 들러 보꾹에 절을 했다. 죽은 자의 유류물을 하도 삼켜

moment you die is when your babe dies, too. It's not fair to your baby if you die now. You understand? You killed that baby so that *you* could live. You've gotta do better than this! "

"If you don't wanna get sick or go mad or shrivel up and die, you can't fear dying. And if you don't want to fear dying, you have to befriend death. Death needs to know why it should let you live. Your dead children saved you. If you don't live, their death is good for nothing. As long as it's not in vain, they still live. If you forget about 'em, you start to fear death, and you wanna run away. Then you become sick and die. And so does the child. Don't run from your fear. Befriend it. Swallow it up and guard it in yourself for a long, long time. Don't forget, you hear? Don't forget!"

No amount of shouting could get them to understand what exactly she was alluding to.

"What should I do not to forget?"

"You gonna do as I say?"

"Of course."

The Myeongdu Lady pointed to the white porcelain jar in the corner.

"Bow to it. Nine times."

She explained:

통통하게 몸이 부푼 명두집이 마을을 돌아다니는 걸 보면 아닌 게 아니라 죽음이 뒤뚱거리며 지나가는 것 같았다. 아낙들은 먼발치서 명두집을 향해 손을 모으거나 조용히 고개를 숙였다. 뒷골엔 그렇게 예전처럼 애들과 가축이 태어났고 죽어갔고, 초목이 베어지고 태워지고 다시 싹을 틔워 꽃을 피웠으며, 사람들은 자라나 병이 들고 병을 고치며 늙어 죽었다. 나도 그사이에 죽었다. 이제 명두집, 그녀가 갈 차례인 것이다.

날이 흐려 초저녁 어둠이 한밤중처럼 깊다. 창문마다 푸른빛이 새어나온다. 그럴싸한 소파에들 앉아 내년에 벌어진다는 국제 축구 경기의 예선전을 보고 있다. 몇 명의 아낙들이 명두집으로 황급히 달려간 사실을 골목의 가로등만 알 뿐이다.

명두집엔 먼 곳에서 소식을 듣고 달려온 아들이 방 한 귀퉁이에 앉아 있다. 어느새 환갑에 이른 그녀의 딸도 장성한 자식들과 함께 어미의 임종을 지킨다.

아낙들이 들이닥치자 아들과 딸이 자리에서 일어선다.

좀 어떠셔요?

한 아낙이 묻는다. 아랫목에 반듯이 누워 있는 명두집

"Y'all would have to come and bow 'til my floors wear out. But I know you women would never do that, so here's what you can do instead. Go home and find me something that the baby wore or the umbilical cord if you have it. I don't need the whole thing, just tear off a piece and bring it to me. I'll swallow it myself and keep it in my body. As long as I'm alive, you'll see me around. When you see me, remember that I carry around the soul of your dead and can take it to the next world at my discretion. Bow to me nine times in your heart and greet me like family. And don't you run away, you hear?"

They followed her instructions and presented her with scraps of baby clothing or pieces of dried umbilical cord. Those with neither brought snippets of the pillows that their babies had used or a pinch of dirt from where their babies had been buried. On both the first and fifteenth day of the lunar month, they deliberately made time to visit the Myeongdu Lady's house and bow to the porcelain jar. Her body had swelled considerably, having swallowed all those relics. When you saw her waddle about the village, it was like watching Death itself pass by. When the women saw her from a dis-

의 눈동자가 천천히 움직인다.

저, 알아보시겠어요?

다른 아낙이 묻는다. 명두집이 희미하게 웃는다.

말씀을 못 하시는가요?

아들을 향해 묻는다. 아들이 말없이 명두집을 바라본다.

나, 이제…… 갈 것이네.

물 밑으로 깊이 가라앉는 명두집의 목소리가 작고 느리고 어둡고 무겁게 들려온다.

이제 우린 어쩐대요?

아낙이 울상이 된다. 명두집이 눈길을 돌려 천장 아래쪽에 붙어 있는 작은 시렁을 오래도록 응시한다. 시렁에 얹혀 있던 백자 항아리를 아들이 조심스레 끌어내린다. 백자 항아리가 명두집 눈길 위에 한동안 머물 수 있도록 아들이 동작을 멈춘다. 명두집이 별다른 반응을 보이지 않자 비로소 바닥에 내려놓는다.

이제들…… 알아서…… 가져가.

어느새 어린 영혼의 것으로 변한 명두집의 목소리가 벌어진 입술 틈새로 힘없이 새어나온다.

한동안 침묵하던 아들이 삼가는 손길로 천천히 봉인

tance, they gathered their hands together and quietly lowered their heads. Life in the old village went on. Children and livestock were born and laid to rest. Trees were cut and fields were burnt, but the earth sprouted vegetation again. The people grew older. They fell ill and recovered and died from old age. I died somewhere in that cycle, too. And now, now it was the Myeongdu Lady's turn to go.

The early evening sky is as dark as night on this overcast day. Blue lights leak out from the windows. The villagers are sitting on decent looking sofas as they watch the qualifying round for the next year's world soccer games. Only the lampposts in the alleys saw the women rush to the Myeongdu Lady's house moments ago.

On hearing the news, the Myeongdu Lady's son had set out immediately for the long trip. He now sits in one corner of the room. Her daughter, close to sixty herself, has come to her mother's deathbed with her grown children.

When the village women scramble in, her son and daughter rise to their feet.

"How are you feeling?" a woman asks the Myeongdu Lady, who lies straight on a warm part of

을 뜯는다. 그러곤 항아리 속 물건들을 하나하나 꺼내 놓는다. 배냇저고리 오린 것, 마른 태반 조각, 베갯잇 조각, 약봉지에 싼 흙, 가느다란 머리카락 몇 올, 플라스틱 딸랑이, 노인의 비녀, 손톱처럼 보이는 것들, 때 묻은 동정 조각, 장갑, 안경집, 반지와 목걸이, 라이터, 그리고 출력한 지 얼마 안 돼 보이는 초음파 태아 사진도 세 장이나 나온다. 그동안 명두집이 삼킨 줄 알았던 망자의 유류품들이다.

아들딸과 나이 든 손자들, 그리고 아낙들이 바닥에 널린 물건들을 바라본다.

이건 뭘까?

한 아낙이 낯선 물건을 집어 든다. 아이의 손가락처럼 생긴 나뭇가지다. 창칼로 껍질을 벗기고 사포로 문질러 표면이 깨끗하다. 하나의 줄기에 세 개의 작은 가지가 뻗은 꼴이다. 포장마차에서 안주로 파는 닭발 같다. 그런 게 세 개나 있다.

명두집은 아무 반응도 보이지 않는다. 그녀는 이미 죽음의 문턱을 막 건너고 있는 것이다. 나는 안다. 아이를 하나씩 묻을 때마다 명두집은 내게서 가지를 꺾어갔다.

the *ondol* floor. Her pupils move slowly towards the voice.

"Do you recognize me?" asks another woman. The Myeongdu Lady smiles faintly.

"Can she still speak?" she asks the Myeongdu Lady's son, who turns to his mother without answering.

"I—I'm going now." She is sinking deep beneath the waters. Her voice is small, slow, dark, and frightening.

"What are we supposed to do now?" A woman bursts into tears. The Myeongdu Lady turns her gaze toward the shelf nailed to the wall. Her son reaches up and carefully lowers the white porcelain jar. He holds it in midair so his mother can keep her eyes on it for a while. Seeing her give no particular response, he sets it down.

"Take—back—what's yours."

Her voice, which had turned into a young soul's once again, just barely slips out from between her lips.

Still silent, her son warily removes the lid. He proceeds to take out the jar's contents one by one. Scraps of baby clothing, pieces of dried cord, snippets of pillow sheets, some dirt in a clear

껍질을 벗겨 다듬었다. 이미 50년 전의 것들이지만 지금 속속들이 검게 죽어 있는 내 가지들에 비하면 살아 있는 것만큼이나 생생하다. 그것이 그녀의 명두였다.

이것들을 다 어떡하라구요.

아낙이 중얼거린다. 명두집은 막 숨을 거둔다.

저 한길에 서 있는 굴참나무는 어쩌구요. 이제 누가 그 나무를 지키나요. 명두님은 어디로 보내드려야 하죠? 나무 밑에 닿아 있는 오솔길도 이제는 풀들로 묻히겠네요. 우리가 대신 그 나무를 찾아 길이 묻히지 않게 할까요?

명두집이 대답할 리 없다.

더 깊어지지 않을 것처럼 밤은 어둡다. 하나둘, 마을의 창문에 불빛이 사라진다. 명두집 창문만 오래도록 꺼지지 않는다. 숨이 멎은 명두집의 낯은 창백하여 차갑지만 백설처럼 평온하다. 그래선지 주검 곁의 사람들은 요란하게 슬퍼하지 않는다.

내 말이 들릴 리도 없겠지만, 어둠을 이고 마을을 보며, 언제나 그랬듯 나는 중얼거린다.

삶을 위해 죽음이 필요한 거였지, 죽음 뒤에까지 죽음

medicine bag, strands of thin hairs, a plastic rattle, a grandmother's hairpin, nail clippings, part of a stained shirt collar, gloves, an eyeglass case, rings and necklaces, a lighter, and three infant ultrasound photos that couldn't have been printed too long ago. All the relics of the deceased are there and not in her stomach as they'd thought.

Her son, daughter, and grandchildren, along with the village women examine the spread.

"I wonder what this is."

A woman picks up an unfamiliar object. It's a small tree limb that looks like a child's fingers. The bark has been stripped off and the rest has been sanded smooth. Three stout twigs extend from out of a thick branch. It resembles a chicken's foot, the kind sold at street vendors. There are three of these.

The Myeongdu Lady shows no reaction at all. She has just stepped over death's threshold. I knew where they came from. Each time she buried a child, the Myeongdu Lady had snapped off one of my branches. She'd stripped away the bark with a knife and had sanded it smooth. They were all well over 50 years old now, but they're as good as living compared to my own rotting branches. Those

이 필요한 건 아닐게요. 그 숱한 명두들과 명두집의 시신은 이제 산 사람들의 소관일 게요. 어떻게 처분되든 우리 죽은 자들에겐 아무래도 상관없는 거라오. 명두집의 숨이 아직 끊어지지 않았더라도 그대들의 마지막 물음엔 그리하여 답하지 않았을 게요. 굳이 저 오솔길이 묻히는 걸 안타까워 말기를. 그대들의 가슴속에 이미 제각기 삶의 길을 품게 됐으니.

『2006 황순원문학상 수상 작품집』, 중앙일보, 2006

were her *myeongdu*—her relics.

"What're we supposed to do with all this?"

The women mutter to themselves. The Myeong-du Lady breathes her last.

"What about that oak tree by the road? Who will protect it now? Where should we lay you, Mrs. Myeongdu? What about the path leading up to the tree? Would you like us to make sure it doesn't disappear?"

The Myeongdu Lady can't answer anymore.

The night is as dark as can be. Throughout the village, the lights in the windows disappear one by one, but the Myeongdu Lady's house stays lit. The Myeongdu Lady is now pale and cold, but her face is at peace, like a bed of new white snow. Perhaps this is why the people surrounding the dead body do not mourn loudly.

The darkness is above me. I know they can't hear me, but I keep speaking my low words to the village, as I always do.

You see, life requires death, but death isn't needed after death. It's now up to the living to decide what to do with the Myeongdu Lady's body and all those relics. But what you do with it no longer concerns us dead. Even if the Myeongdu Lady had

heard your last questions, she wouldn't have offered any instructions. And please, don't feel sorry
about neglecting our path. In your hearts, you've
already started laying your own.

Translated by Michelle Jooeun Kim

해설

Afterword

'살아남음'의 책임에 대하여

류수연 (문학평론가)

　　구효서의「명두」는 굴참나무의 목소리를 통해 명두집의 삶을 되짚어 나가는 독특한 시점을 가진 작품이다. 명두는 본래 놋으로 만든 무당들의 신구(神具) 혹은 그 안에 깃든 혼령을 지칭하는 말이다. 이는 이승을 떠나지 못한 혼령의 살아생전 한(恨)이 사물에 깃들면, 그 자체로 영험한 능력이 된다는 믿음 위에 기초한다. 명두집이 '명두집'이라 불리게 된 이유는 소리 소문 없이 태어났다 죽어버린 그녀의 세 아이 때문이었다. 죽은 아이를 땅에 묻지 않고 옹기에 담아 명두로 삼았다는 낭설은, 어느 순간 범접할 수 없는 위엄을 갖게 된 명두집에 대한 경외를 정당화한다.

On the Responsibility of "Surviving"

Ryu Su-yun (literary critic)

"Relics" by Ku Hyo-seo is a unique, innovative piece, a story of a woman known only as the Myeongdu Lady and narrated by nothing other than an old oak tree. The word *myeongdu* in Korean refers to a magical copper talisman commonly utilized by shamans. Based on the premise that souls of the dead could enter objects if they failed to depart, these *myeongdu* were believed to lend miraculous powers to their owners. In Ku Hyo-seo's singularly moving *Relics,* his Myeongdu Lady earns her name because people believe she has used her own dead children as the source of her powers.

In a sense, these rumors do prove to be half true,

그러나 그것은 절반의 사실일 뿐이다. 그녀의 세 아이가 죽은 것은 사실이었으나, 그 아이들이 묻힌 곳은 옹기가 아니라 백오십 년 된 굴참나무 아래였기 때문이다. 그럼에도 불구하고 "묵살했다가는 이승은 물론 저승에서마저 반드시 급살귀신이 되게 할 것 같은 그녀의 무시무시한 서슬"을 만들어낸 것은 바로 그 세 아이이다. 그것은 원혼이 명두가 되었기 때문이 아니다. 죽은 아이들을 잊지 않고 기억함으로써 그들의 죽음을 자기 삶의 일부로 만들고자 했던 명두집의 염원이야말로, 그녀 자신을 "죽음이 뒤뚱거리며 지나가는 것"과 같은 존재로 만들었던 것이다. 식지 않은 세 아이의 주검을 위해 무덤이 되어주었던 굴참나무만이 그녀의 비밀을 지켜주는 유일한 존재가 된다.

　이러한 명두집의 삶은 혹독했던 전후의 현실 위에서 조형된다. 가난으로 인해 두 아이를 굴참나무 아래 묻었고, 남편을 잃고 전쟁통에 마을 남정네들에게 겁간당하며 아비도 모르는 아이를 낳아 또 다시 두 아이의 곁에 묻어야 했다. 그럼에도 불구하고 그녀는 죽지 않고 살아남았다. 너무나 무력했던 그녀가 변화한 것은 세 번째 아이를 굴참나무 밑에 묻으면서였다. 죽은 세

but, of course, the exact nature and significance of her mythical status go far beyond that. Midway through the old tree's story the reader discovers the Myeongdu Lady's children have indeed died. They were also, it turns out, buried under the 150-year-old oak tree itself. Regardless, the villagers attribute the protagonist's "terrible aura" that "threatened to turn anyone who went against her wishes into a sinister phantom in this life and the next life" to her three children and their burial ground. Death's unmistakable presence about her turns her into a terrifying specter. The villagers describe seeing her as "like watching Death itself pass by." Only the oak tree that has become the grave for the still-warm infants know her secret: It is her desire to incorporate their death into her life, her remembrance of their deaths rather than their early passing that sources her powers.

And it turns out that this life has not been an easy one. The Myeongdu Lady's life is thoroughly grounded in harsh post-war realities. Like so many other mothers in her village, post-war poverty leaves her unable to sustain her first two children. She is left with no other choice but to watch them slowly expire and then bury them under the oak.

아이를 잊지 않겠다는 노력이, 그녀를 생존하게 만든 것이다.

"죽음은 끝없이 생명을 만들고, 삶은 끝없이 죽음을 낳았다." 사람들이 살기 위해서라는 미명 아래 수많은 죽음을 잊어가는 동안에도, "명두집은 잊지 않았다. 50년 동안 하루도 잊은 날이 없었다." '잊지 않음'은 세 아이를 죽이고 살아남아야 했던 명두집의 생존에 대한 책임이었다. 그것은 때때로 떠올리다 어느 순간 잊어버리는 소극적인 기억이 아니다. 살아가는 모든 순간 끊임없이 죽음의 의미를 자기 삶의 가장 중요한 자리에 놓고자 노력하는 적극적인 책임으로서의 기억이다. 이 기억이 만들어내는 주술적인 힘이야말로 죽은 굴참나무가 살아서 이야기할 수 있는 동력이며, 사다리도 없는 철탑에 올라가 쓰러진 청년을 구해낸 명두집의 기적 같은 균형감각을 가능하게 만든 힘이었다. 죽음을 기억하며, 그것과 함께 하는 자만이 죽음을 두려워하지 않을 수 있는 것이다. 명두집은 그녀를 둘러싼 모든 죽음을 기억하는 데 자기 삶의 시간을 할애함으로써, '살아남음'의 책임을 다한 삶을 살았다. 만약 그녀에게 명두가 있다면, 이 기억이야말로 진정한 명두라고 할 수 있다.

Then, after her husband dies, the men in the village repeatedly take advantage of her, and she gives birth once again. Not even aware of the father's identity, she buries this child next to her other children for the last time. Though weak and powerless to resist her circumstances until this point, it is here that Ku's protagonist finally decides things will change.

For the Myeongdu Lady, it becomes her responsibility as a mother and murderer of her own children to survive in order not to forget. "Death created life to no end, and life gave birth to death in the same manner." While the majority of villagers have forgotten about their children and family whom they have long since allowed to die, "the Myeongdu Lady absolutely refuses this course of action. Not a day in 50 years did she forget." The act of not forgetting becomes for her, not a passive act involving remembering from time to time, forgetting everything eventually. Rather, her act of not forgetting requires the constant effort of giving the death the most important place in her life. The mystical powers conjured by this kind of remembrance explains how a dead oak tree can narrate stories and how the Myeongdu Lady is later able to

이는 이 소설의 가장 빛나는 부분이다. 여기엔 모성신화로 쉽게 포장될 수 없는 그 '무엇'이 있다. 모진 세월 속에서 스스로 세 아이를 묻어야 했고, 그렇게 살아남은 그녀가 짊어진 삶의 무게는 모성의 그것보다 크고 무거웠다. 죽음이 두렵지 않은 그녀의 현재는 죽음보다 끔찍한 생의 굴곡을 거쳐 완성된 것이기 때문이다. 그 힘을 작가는 "불망(不忘)"이라는 단어의 주술로서 환기한다. 기억한다는 것. 사실 그것은 얼마나 끔찍한 형벌인가? 자신에게 찾아오는 병자들에게 '불망'을 외치는 명두집은 살기 위함이라는 핑계 속에 은폐된 혹은 묵인된 죄책감을 일깨운다. 살기 위해 행한 모든 악행을 기억하고 결코 잊지 않는 것이야말로 인간이 감내해야 할 형벌이라고 말하고 있는 것이다.

이처럼 「명두」는 삶과 죽음이라는 보편적인 문제의식을 다루는 동시에, 생존의 의미를 진지하게 고민하는 구효서만의 날카로움을 놓치지 않은 수작이다. 그는 수많은 죽음을 끌어안고 지탱함으로써 완성되는 명두집의 삶을 통해, 보편성이라는 말로 아우를 수 없는 화두를 오늘의 독자에게 던지고 있다. 그것은 '살아남음'의 책임이다. 항아리 속에 봉인되었던 수많은 망자의 유류

walk across a narrow steel beam to rescue the young man. Remembering death and the pride that comes from it allows one face death without fear. By taking time out of her life to remember all the deaths she has experienced, she carries out her responsibility of "surviving" to the fullest. If Ku's protagonist does indeed possess a *myeongdu*, it is her act of remembering.

It is perhaps, this turning point of Ku's heroine that stands out the most. Her almost vengeful new course of action in life adds another dimension to what could otherwise be explained as the transcendental powers of mothers. The Myeongdu Lady's burden of living—from having to bury three of her own children, is much heavier than the normal burden of mothers. Her present life—a life no longer accompanied by the fear of death—is the outcome of living through circumstances more awful than dying. Ku has his character chant "Don't forget" to explain the source of her strength. In a sense, remembering is actually her terrible punishment. The Myeongdu Lady tells her patients not to forget in order to arouse their guilt, whether it be hidden or excused, from within. Always remembering and never forgetting the wrongs committed

품들은, 원혼 때문이 아니라 그 모든 죽음을 자기 삶에 축적하고자 했던 명두집으로 인해 영험한 명두로 거듭 날 수 있었다. 따라서 「명두」에서 명두는 죽은 자를 가둔 감옥이 아닌, 죽어서 또 다시 살게 만드는 절실한 소통의 출발이 된다.

그리하여 구효서는 굴참나무의 목소리를 빌려 오늘의 독자를 각성시킨다. 삶을 위해 죽음이 필요하다면, 그 죽음을 '불망'하는 것이야말로 살아남은 자들의 책임이라고.

in order to live becomes the very punishment for those wrongs.

At the same time, Ku's new story deals with universal issues of life and death. *Relics* is also a heavy contemplation of the meaning and implications of dogged survival in the face of impossible odds. Through the life of a woman who has accepted and sustained countless deaths, Ku Hyo-seo presents a tale that the word "universal" falls short in describing. Ku's story expounds upon the *responsibility* of surviving. The relics of the deceased stored inside the jar served as *myeongdu*, not because of the tragic deaths associated with them, but because of the Myeongdu Lady's efforts to incorporate these deaths into her life. The souls of the deceased are not caged up within objects. Rather, the objects serve as a medium of communication for death to have life again.

Ku Hyo-seo borrows the voice of an oak tree to awaken today's audience. If death is needed for life, the old oak seems to say, it is the responsibility of those who live to remember and never to forget.

비평의 목소리

Critical Acclaim

구효서는 '전업작가'라는 말이 어색했던 그 시절부터 지금껏 '전업작가'로서의 순결성을 지키고 있는 드문 사례로, 등단(1987년) 이래 가시적인 시대이념과 지향이 사라지는 시간들, 문학이 점차 왜소해져간 시간들을 소설 쓰는 일과 함께 겪어왔다. 작가 스스로 여러 번 밝힌 바 있듯이, 그에게 소설은 함께 살고 늙어가고 소멸해갈 동반자이자 그의 존재를 되비치는 거울 자체다. 그러므로 여기에는 소설이 시대이념이나 문예이론을 세속화한 장소라거나 문학적 개성을 실험하는 자유공간이라는 의식이 철저히 배제되어 있다. 소설로 일상을 채우고 생계를 꾸리는 그에게 소설은 천박한 삶과 유리

Ku Hyo-seo became a "full-time writer" when the term itself began to raise eyebrows. Since receiving this particular critical acclaim, Ku has not compromised his title to this day. Since his literary debut in 1987, Ku has written during periods where more concrete ideology and aspirations have receded and where the significance of literature gradually has lost weight. As he himself revealed, the novel to Ku is a companion with whom he wants to share life, grow old, and disappear. It is a mirror that reflects his being. His novels, therefore, are not platforms to secularize current ideologies or literary theories, nor are they free spaces for lit-

된 숭고한 어떤 것도, 문제적 세계와 만나는 통로도 아니며 한 개인의 감정의 배출구는 더더욱 아니다. 일상이자 작가 자신에 대한 성찰이 곧 그의 소설이며, 어쩌면 소설이 그의 삶을 쓰고 있다는 표현이 좀 더 정확하다고도 할 수 있을 것이다.

소영현, 「일상이자 성찰인 글/쓰기」, 《창비》, 2006 봄호, 342쪽.

구효서 소설의 인물들은 대개 어떤 경계 위에 있다. 삶과 죽음, 현재와 과거, 존재와 부재, 일상과 탈일상, 세속과 탈속 등등의 경계가 바로 그것이다. 그곳은 각기 상반하는 두 세계가 등을 맞대고 있는 지점이면서 동시에 어느 순간 그 둘이 서로 넘나들고 교통하는 '사건'이 발생하는 지점이다.

김영찬, 해설 「그늘 속으로, 허무와 탈아(脫我)의 윤리」,

『시계가 걸렸던 자리』, 창비, 2005, 271쪽.

「명두」는 죽은 굴참나무의 목소리로 서술된다. "나는 죽었다"라는 문장으로 시작되는 이 소설은 서두에서부터 죽은 것의 '살아있음'을 증명하는 듯하다. 뿐만 아니라 이 나무가 이야기하고 있는 명두집은 마을 사람들에

erary experimentation. As someone who sustains himself and fills his day-to-day with writing, novels are more than noble entities set apart from the cruelty of life. Nor are they channels to meet a problematic world, and certainly not mere outlets for his emotions. His novels are reflections of his daily life as well as of himself. It might even be safe to say that his novels write his story instead of the reverse.

So Young-hyun, "Writing as Daily Life and Introspection," *The Quarterly Changbi*, Spring 2006, 342.

Most of the characters in Ku Hyo-seo's stories straddle some sort of border, whether they be between life and death, present and past, existence and absence, daily life and their escape, or the world and the otherworldly. Ku's stories exist at the point where two conflicting worlds stand back to back, but at the same time it becomes the point where the two intersect and "happenings" can occur.

Kim Young-chan, "Commentary: Into the Shade, Ethics of Futility and Escaping Self," *Where the Clock Once Hung* (Paju: Changbi, 2005), 271.

게 죽음을 삼킨 '걸어다니는 사자'로 여겨졌고, 그래서 그녀를 보면 사람들은 "죽음이 뒤뚱거리며 지나가는 것" 같다며 손을 모으거나 고개를 숙였다고 하니, 명두집은 그야말로 '살아있는 죽음' 그 자체였던 셈이다. 이 소설에서 죽음이란 삶 저편에 자리한 것도, 두려워하며 도망쳐야 할 대상도 아니다. 명두집의 말처럼 "도망치거나 잊지 말고 그놈과 평생 함께 살아야" 하는 것이다. '죽은 나무의 말하기'는 그 자체로 이런 죽음의 '살아있음'을 보여준다.

황도경, 「꽃이 되는 어둠, 그곳에 달이 있다」, 《창비》,

2009 겨울호, 431쪽.

"불망!" 이 소설을 지탱하고 있는 뿌리 말이다. "잊는게 죽는 거라구." 그렇다면 무얼 잊어서는 안 된다는 걸까? 절실. 살기 위해 자신들의 갓난아이를 묻어야 했던 그 절실함을 잊지 않는 것. 그래서 가난한 '툇골' 마을을 살아서 150년, 죽어서 20년을 지켜보고 있는 '굴참나무'가 들려주듯 "그대들의 가슴속에 이미 제가끔 삶의 길을 품"는 것. 그것이 '명두집'이 우리에게 들려주는 절실의 내실(內室/內實)이다.

"Relics" is narrated by a dead oak tree. From its very first line, "I am dead," the story seeks to prove that death also has life. Furthermore, the tree tells the story of the Myeongdu Lady, who the villagers considered a walking dead person, a being that has swallowed death. They gathered their hands and bow their heads at the sight of her. For the villagers it is like "watching Death itself pass by." It seemed she was, indeed, the walking dead. In this novel, death is not some unknown entity on the other side of life, nor is it something to run away from in fear. In the words of the Myeongdu Lady, "Don't run away." The fact that a dead tree is able to speak, too, shows that death can also live.

Hwang Do-kyung, "Where Darkness Blooms, There is the Moon," *The Quarterly Changbi*, Winter 2009, 431.

"Do not forget!" This command sustains this novel. "When you forget, you die." What is she telling them not to forget? Desperation. She tells them not to forget the desperation that leaves them with no choice but to bury their infant children. As an oak tree that once guarded the poor village for 150 years alive and then for 20 years dead points out, they've "already started to lay their own [paths]" in

유준, 「절실의 내실(內室/內實)」, 《문학과사회》,

2009 겨울호, 447쪽.

　구효서 소설의 주요 화두가 되어 왔던 '죽음'은 이 소설에 이르러 한 개인의 실존적 차원을 넘어 역사와 집단의 테제로 확장되고 있다. 작가는 단편소설이 감당하기 쉽지 않은 긴 역사의 시간과 근대소설이 떠나온 무속의 세계까지 끌어들이면서 삶과 죽음이 서로의 꼬리를 물고 이어지는 선악의 경계 없는 자연의 리듬이 궁극에서는 이 근대의 시간과 인간사의 현실에 엄연히 개재해 있음을 새삼 확인시키는데, (……) 명두집의 사연을 통해 작가가 제기하는 '불망(不忘)'의 윤리는 삶과 죽음이 한 몸으로 이어진 자연의 시간에 맞서, 그것을 감싸 인간의 시간과 역사를 성찰하고 의미 있게 만드는 기억해둘 만한 테제가 아니겠는가.

　정홍수, 해설 「소설의 조율과 승경의 발견」, 『저녁이 아름다운 집』,

랜덤하우스코리아, 2009, 309~310쪽.

life. That is the inner desperation that *Relics* alludes to.

Yoo Joon, "Substance of Being Earnest," *Literature and Society*, Winter 2009, 447.

Death has been a major issue in Ku Hyo-seo's novels. In this particular story, death goes beyond the existential dimension of the individual; it is expanded as a thesis encompassing history and society. The writer accomplishes a difficult feat for a short story by bringing together history and the shamanistic world that contemporary novels have long abandoned. Ku demonstrates that life and death have each other at their tails—that the cycle of nature, absent of good and evil, allows for contemporary time to remain interposed within the reality of human history. [...] The ethics of "not forgetting" is a thesis that gives significance to the time and history of humans in the face of natural time, a realm where life and death constitute one body.

Jeong Hong-su, "Commentary: Tuning of a Story and Discovery of the Picturesque," *The House with a Beautiful Evening* (Seoul: Random House Korea, 2009), 309-10.

구효서

작가 구효서는 1957년 9월 18일 경기도 강화군 하점
면 창후리에서 태어났다. 1972년 갑작스럽게 상경하면
서 당산동에 소재한 영도 중학교를 졸업했다. 작가는
이 갑작스러운 이향과 낯선 도시에서의 삶이 그에게서
표정을 빼앗았다고 고백하기도 한다. 그의 본격적인 습
작기는 재수를 하던 1977년 무렵이다. 친구들과 어울려
〈난필지변(亂筆之辯)〉이라는 시 동인지를 만들면서 시
작한 습작은, 1978년 목원대학교 국어교육과에 입학한
이후에도 꾸준히 이어진다. 시인 김요섭의 권고로 대학
시절부터는 산문에 집중하게 된다. 여러 번의 신춘문예
낙방을 거치던 그는, 1987년 《중앙일보》 신춘문예에 단
편 「마디」가 당선되어 본격적으로 작품 활동을 시작한
다. 1991년 5월 3일 전업 작가로 살겠다고 선언한 이후,
작품 창작에 몰입하여 다양한 작품을 발표하며 문단의
주목을 받게 된다. 1994년 한국일보문학상을 수상한
「깡통따개가 없는 마을」은 90년대를 대표하는 작품으
로 평가받는다. 80년대 문학이 격렬한 민주화 투쟁 속

Ku Hyo-seo

Ku Hyo-seo was born on September 18, 1957 in the Gyeonggi-do Province (Ganghwa-gun, Hajeom-myeon, Changhu-ri). After an unexpected move to Seoul in 1972, he graduated from Yeongdo Middle School in Dangsan-dong. He later confessed that the sudden departure from his hometown and life in an unfamiliar city seemed to steal all expression from his face. He wrote as a hobby and started a literary coterie magazine with his high-school friends called "Nanpiljibyeon" in 1977. He continued to write after he entered Mokwon University where he studied Korean Language and Education. Following the recommendation of poet Kim Yo-seop, he began to focus on prose-writing in college. After several rejected submissions, his short story "Madi" won the *Joongang Ilbo*'s annual literary contest in 1987. After declaring himself as a full-time writer on May 3, 1991, a variety of works were published and he began to gain attention in literary circles. *Village Without a Can-Opener* won the *Hankook Ilbo* Literary Award in 1994 and is now often

에서 공동체의 문제에 집중했다면, 90년대 문학은 고도의 자본주의 성장과 대중문화의 전방위적 확산 속에서 어느 순간 홀로 남겨진 개인의 문제로 눈을 돌린다. 구효서는 진중하게 개인의 내면을 탐사하는 일련의 작품을 발표하면서, 인간에 대한 깊은 통찰을 통해 자칫 사변적일 수 있는 서사적 한계를 극복해낸다.

　그러나 구효서는 자신의 세계를 90년대라는 시대적 조건 속에 가두지 않았다. 오히려 그의 작품 활동은 2000년대 들어서면서 더욱 깊어진다. 개인의 내면에 대한 탐색을 멈추지 않으면서도, 보다 능동적으로 한국 현대사의 수많은 굴곡들을 개인의 삶이라는 결 위에 풀어놓는다. 더 나아가 삶과 죽음이라는 보편적인 주제 안에서 인간과 역사, 그리고 운명에 대한 보다 깊이 있는 천착을 보여주고 있다. 2005년 「소금가마니」로 이효석문학상 수상, 2006년 「명두」로 황순원문학상 수상, 2007년 「시계가 걸렸던 자리」로 한무숙문학상 수상, 2007년 「조율-피아노 월인천강지곡」으로 허균문학작가상, 2008년 『나가사키 파파』로 대산문학상을 수상하며, 그는 2000년대에도 여전히 가장 동시대적인 작가로서 한국문학의 생생한 중심에 서게 된다.

cited as a piece highly representative of Korea in the 1990s. Whereas Korean literature in the '80s focused on collective issues that surfaced during the fierce battle for democracy, literature in the '90s turned its attention to the individual suddenly left alone in face of a fiercely changing capitalism and popular culture. The series of pieces he presented in that period probed deep into the interior of the individual. His insights into basic humanity are often described as overcoming narrative limitations that one might easily perceive as speculative.

Ku Hyo-seo did not confine his aims to '90s-era fiction, however. His writing grew even deeper after the turn of the century. While still continuing his examination of the individual, he began to more actively unravel questions of modern Korean history along with the life of the individual. Under universal themes of life and death, Ku's writing has continued to inquire deep into the universal themes of humanity, history, and fate.

During the first decade of the new millennium, Ku has taken his place at the center of Korean literature as a preeminently relevant writer of his times. His award-winning works include: "Bag of Salt" (2005, Yi Hyo-seok Literary Award), "Relics" (2006,

소설집에『노을은 다시 뜨는가』『확성기가 있었고 저격병이 있었다』『깡통따개가 없는 마을』『그녀의 야윈 뺨』『도라지꽃 누님』『아침 깜짝 물결무늬 풍뎅이』『시계가 걸렸던 자리』『저녁이 아름다운 집』『별명의 달인』등이, 장편소설에『늪을 건너는 법』『슬픈 바다』『전장의 겨울』『추억되는 것의 아름다움 혹은 슬픔』『낯선 여름』『라디오 라디오』『비밀의 문』『남자의 서쪽』『내 목련 한 그루』『오남리 이야기』『악당 임꺽정』『몌별』『애별』『나가사키 파파』『랩소디 인 베를린』『타락』등이 있으며, 산문집에『인생은 지나간다』『인생은 깊어간다』가 있다.

Hwang Sun-won Literary Award), "Where the Clock Hung" (2007, Han Mu-suk Literary Award), "Tuning—Piano Weolincheongangjigok" (2007, Heo Kyun Literary Writer's Award), and *Nagasaki Papa* (2008, Daesan Literary Award).

Also, his short story collections include: *Will the Sunset Come Again; A Loudspeaker and a Sniper; Village Without a Can Opener; Her Thin Cheeks; Bellflower Sister; Morning Surprise Beetle; Where the Clock Hung; The Home With a Beautiful Evening;* and *The Master of Nicknames.*

He has written a number of full length novels: *How to Cross a Swamp; The Sad Ocean; A Winter of Combat; The Beauty and Sadness of Memories; An Unfamiliar Summer; Radio, Radio; Secret Door; The West of a Man; My Magnolia Tree; Story of Onam Village; Outlaw Im Kkeok-jeong; Sad Parting; Grievous Parting; Nagasaki Papa; Rhapsody in Berlin;* and *Corruption.*

Finally, his prose collections include *Life Passes* and *Life Deepens.*

번역 **미셸 주은 김** Translated by Michelle Jooeun Kim

미셸 주은 김(김주은)은 버지니아 주립대학교 국제학과를 졸업하고 한동대학교 통역번역대학원에서 석사학위를 받았다. 이승우 단편소설 「칼」의 번역으로 한국문학번역원 제11회 한국문학번역신인상을 수상하였다.

Michelle Jooeun Kim studied Foreign Affairs at the University of Virginia and received her master's degree in Applied Linguistics and Translation at Handong University's Graduate School of Interpretation and Translation. She received the 11th Korean Literature Translation Award for New Translators with Lee Seung-u's short story "The Knife."

감수 **전승희, 데이비드 윌리엄 홍**

Edited by Jeon Seung-hee and David William Hong

전승희는 서울대학교와 하버드대학교에서 영문학과 비교문학으로 박사 학위를 받았으며, 현재 하버드대학교 한국학 연구소의 연구원으로 재직하며 아시아 문예 계간지 《ASIA》 편집위원으로 활동 중이다. 현대 한국문학 및 세계문학을 다룬 논문을 다수 발표했으며, 바흐친의 『장편소설과 민중언어』, 제인 오스틴의 『오만과 편견』 등을 공역했다. 1988년 한국여성연구소의 창립과 《여성과 사회》의 창간에 참여했고, 2002년부터 보스턴 지역 피학대 여성을 위한 단체인 '트랜지션하우스' 운영에 참여해 왔다. 2006년 하버드대학교 한국학 연구소에서 '한국 현대사와 기억'을 주제로 한 워크숍을 주관했다.

Jeon Seung-hee is a member of the Editorial Board of *ASIA*, is a Fellow at the Korea Institute, Harvard University. She received a Ph.D. in English Literature from Seoul National University and a Ph.D. in Comparative Literature from Harvard University. She has presented and published numerous papers on modern Korean and world literature. She is also a co-translator of Mikhail Bakhtin's *Novel and the People's Culture* and Jane Austen's *Pride and Prejudice*. She is a founding member of the Korean Women's Studies Institute and of the biannual Women's Studies' journal *Women and Society* (1988), and she has been working at 'Transition House,' the first and oldest shelter for battered women in New England. She organized a workshop entitled "The Politics of Memory in Modern Korea" at the Korea Institute, Harvard University, in 2006. She also served as an advising committee member for the Asia-Africa Literature Festival in 2007 and for the POSCO Asian Literature Forum in 2008.

데이비드 윌리엄 홍은 미국 일리노이주 시카고에서 태어났다. 일리노이대학교에서 영문학을, 뉴욕대학교에서 영어교육을 공부했다. 지난 2년간 서울에 거주하면서 처음으로 한국인과 아시아계 미국인 문학에 깊이 몰두할 기회를 가졌다. 현재 뉴욕에서 거주하며 강의와 저술 활동을 한다.

David William Hong was born in 1986 in Chicago, Illinois. He studied English Literature at the University of Illinois and English Education at New York University. For the past two years, he lived in Seoul, South Korea, where he was able to immerse himself in Korean and Asian-American literature for the first time. Currently, he lives in New York City, teaching and writing.

바이링궐 에디션 한국 대표 소설 078

명두

2014년 11월 14일 초판 1쇄 발행

지은이 구효서 | 옮긴이 미셸 주은 김 | 펴낸이 김재범
감수 전승희, 데이비드 윌리엄 홍 | 기획위원 정은경, 전성태, 이경재
편집 정수인, 이은혜, 김형욱, 윤단비 | 관리 박신영 | 디자인 이춘희
펴낸곳 (주)아시아 | 출판등록 2006년 1월 27일 제406-2006-000004호
주소 서울특별시 동작구 서달로 161-1(흑석동 100-16)
전화 02.821.5055 | 팩스 02.821.5057 | 홈페이지 www.bookasia.org
ISBN 979-11-5662-049-5 (set) | 979-11-5662-052-5 (04810)
값은 뒤표지에 있습니다.

Bi-lingual Edition Modern Korean Literature 078

Relics

Written by Ku Hyo-seo | **Translated by** Michelle Jooeun Kim
Published by Asia Publishers | 161-1, Seodal-ro, Dongjak-gu, Seoul, Korea
Homepage Address www.bookasia.org | **Tel**. (822).821.5055 | **Fax**. (822).821.5057
First published in Korea by Asia Publishers 2014
ISBN 979-11-5662-049-5 (set) | 979-11-5662-052-5 (04810)